THE SIMMONS PAPERS

*

*

THE
SIMMONS PAPERS

EDITED AND WITH AN INTRODUCTION

BY

PHILIPP BLOM

faber and faber

LONDON · BOSTON

First published in 1995
by Faber and Faber Limited
3 Queen Square London WC1N 3AU

Phototypeset by Intype Ltd, London
Printed and bound in Great Britain by
Mackays of Chatham PLC, Chatham, Kent

A CIP record for this book is available from the British Library

ISBN 0 571 17315 2

2 4 6 8 10 9 7 5 3 1

*

for
Veronica

INTRODUCTION

*

*Scholarship is concerned with describing realities.
But it is not only since Heisenberg that we know that
it is impossible to observe a system without changing
its state. By describing realities we invent them.*

P. E. H. SIMMONS, Scrapbooks, NR 342.

THE MANUSCRIPT which is here for the first time published
outside a scholarly journal has by now acquired a certain
fame, not to say notoriety, among scholars of language and
philosophy. It appeared first as a whole in the *Journal for
Theology and Literature* (Oxford University Press, 1987, Nr 3,
pp. 321–85) and was immediately regarded as somewhat
sensational, both by philosophers interested in Simmons'
later development, and by literary scholars. When the
papers were found among the thousands of notes and files
which Simmons had assembled during a lifetime of scholarship, little was known about their importance, and a considerable time went by before it came to the attention of
anyone who was in a position to appreciate them properly.

To the student of philosophy the name of Simmons
hardly needs an introduction; however, the layman may be
interested to learn about the life of this extraordinary figure,
perhaps the most underestimated and original thinker of his
generation, which is here sketched out in the barest detail

(a comprehensive and satisfactory biography is still to be
written, and is eagerly awaited).

P. E. H. SIMMONS (1901–1989)

*

PAUL EDWARD HEINRICH SIMMONS was born on 22 January 1901, the only son of Edward Mortimer Simmons, KC, a man of gentle breeding (Winchester and New College), and his wife Henriette, née Hintermeier, of Leipzig, Germany. Edward Simmons, a senior judge, had taken his second wife Henriette, to the great surprise of his friends and relations, after a sojourn at Karlsbad in 1899, to which town she had come in the service of the Duke of Saxony-Altenburg as lady-in-waiting and future governess (she was never to work as a governess for the duke, since she left for Britain to marry Edward six months before the heir to the duchy, Georg Moritz, was born in 1900). The marriage proved to be a happy one, and Paul was tutored at home by his mother before being sent at the age of thirteen to his father's old college. He had to leave Winchester in 1915, his father having been forced into an early retirement on account of the growing hostility towards his German wife, to whom he remained devotedly loyal. The family found itself under a marked financial strain, and so Paul, after an unhappy spell at Abingdon College for Boys, returned to the tuition of his mother. The events of his childhood may account in part for Simmons' life-long ambivalent stance toward English traditions and society, which expressed itself at times in uncompromising and often acid comments. In an attempt to prove his loyalty to Empire, which he later came to call 'misguided, pointless and naïve', he volunteered for the army and fought in France and Belgium from 1917 to 1918. He returned from the war with an injured knee, which compelled him to use a walking-stick thenceforth. Regarding his injury, he remarked sardonically that it had been caused 'not by German shrapnel on the battlefield, but by a tramway in one of the less respectable districts of Paris'.

Having won a scholarship to Merton College, Oxford, with which he was to form a lasting attachment, Simmons went up in 1920 to read history, but changed to philosophy in his second year. His solid knowledge of both subjects made him a close associate of R. G. Collingwood, who confessed to having been led to many of the ideas which were to form his 'Idea of History' in discussions with his student, whose gifts he was the first to recognize. After completing his BA, Simmons went to the University of Vienna, which was then a leading centre for studies in philosophy. There he studied with, among others, Moritz von Schlick. The grounding in continental philosophical traditions which Simmons received there gave him later a unique authority in Oxford, but at the same time condemned him to a peripheral role in developments within the faculty, a fact further aggravated by the scorn exhibited towards him by the eminent analytical philosopher Alfred Ayer. Simmons' controversial views were also evident in his attitude to Wittgenstein, whom he regarded as hopelessly over-estimated. (Simmons is said to have remarked that he would have made a passable engineer if he had cared to get his qualification in Berlin.) In 1931, Simmons won a fellowship to Balliol, a position which he held until his death. In the ensuing years he became a well known and highly respected tutor and teacher and an authority on the metaphysical tradition. His expertise in this area led, in 1935, to his appointment as Waynflete Professor, the youngest man for almost two hundred years to hold this post. The rise in anti-German feeling openly exhibited towards him by older members of the faculty led him to resign from this post only three months later. (The position was then taken up by Collingwood, his friend and former teacher.)

After his resignation Simmons declined to accept any further position, but never moved away from Oxford, despite numerous offers from other universities in Britain and abroad.

The remaining forty years of his life were spent in relative obscurity, unknown to any but a small and constant number of tutees and old friends. This time can be regarded as philosophically the most fruitful of his life. It was during these years that he wrote the works which made him a revered figure for a select circle of philosophers in Europe, long before he became fashionable in American universities: a volume of revised early essays, the study *Cusanus and the Doctrine of Non-Existent Being*, *The Vienna Circle* (a survey of the philosophical developments in Vienna in the 1920s, now regarded as the authoritative text on the subject), a monograph on the philosophical implications of lexicography, and his magnum opus, *Philosophy of Names in Europe after W. v. Humbold*. After 1984 he finally started work on his 'scrapbooks', which were published posthumously, and are arguably the most enigmatic piece of philosophy since Heidegger's *Sein und Zeit*. Having been prone to depression from his early adolescence, Simmons had an especialy difficult time between 1954 and 1957, when one of his students, to whom he had become personally attached, suddenly died in a motor accident. After this time he became markedly eccentric, and refused to receive visitors who were not personally known to him. This perhaps explains the fact that there are no recorded interviews with him, nor even any philosophical epigones who can claim a personal connection.

Depression was to haunt Simmons throughout his life. Following his departure from Abingdon College on account of the several fits he suffered there, it ceased for several decades, only to return with renewed force when he was fifty-three, never to leave him again. At times the 'black days', as he referred to them in his diaries, became so overwhelming that Simmons had to be taken into institutional care for weeks on end. At such times he lived in complete isolation, but for the medical visits he received and a caretaker who brought him the daily papers. He is reported to have worked during these periods with a manic persistence on a manuscript which he would not let anybody see, consulting dictionaries of several different languages.

The changes which Oxford underwent during Simmons'

life were the cause of many comments by him which have passed into folklore among Oxford fellows who deplore the recent developments. His statement that Oxford had 'by no means become more open or even better, only more suburban and generally less cultured' led to a virulent public attack upon him by a young literary critic who accused him of adopting a politically incorrect attitude, and of evident racism and elitism. While Simmons' unfashionable statements alienated him from the architects of reform, the current student population was equally antagonized by them. With characteristic forthrightness he compared the present students unfavourably with those of Oxford's 'golden age' (his own time, and that of many other great Oxford personalities). In his view, the former matched the latter 'certainly in arrogance, but not remotely in wit and style'.

Recriminations and misunderstanding did not bother him in the least, nor was he unduly fastidious in avoiding delicate topics of conversation. He was known to enjoy the spectacle of others struggling to steer an argument away from perilous waters to less disconcerting subjects in the attempt to avoid embarrassment, a phenomenon which he called 'the blackest English horror, more feared than famine, death and war'.

It is surprising how a staunchly conservative Englishman (if one with subversive, almost anarchistic leanings) could ever become a fashionable figure in the academic community of the United States, yet this is exactly what happened. Interest in Simmons was triggered by the article

'Intuitionism, the Game of Coherency and the Dignity of Fiction: Paul Simmons and Robert Musil', which was published in *Language and Speech* (Harvard, 1984) and written by the two young American scholars, J. B. Klootzak and B. F. Levine. The article was a sensation in literary criticism, and Simmons' works rapidly became popular subjects of debate, in particular his work on the philosophy of names. The ensuing flurry of invitations, seminars, lectures, and two congresses (Harvard, 1986; Atlanta, 1988) left Simmons unimpressed. Not only did he refuse to accept any invitation to lecture in America, but he made no secret of the fact that he considered the discussion there to be 'beside the point, illiterate, and totally meretricious'. It is related that one academic, not to be deterred by the lack of response to his overtures, came personally to see Simmons at Balliol. On being asked whether he read Latin, he was obliged to respond in the negative, whereupon it was suggested that he go home at once and set about learning it.

Simmons adopted the same outspoken and almost offensive position towards academic institutions, refusing outright honorary doctorates from the universities of Vienna and Wuppertal. Arguing that he had no merit in the field which was to honour him, he added caustically that neither university held a scholar competent to judge him. His uncompromising attitude to formal honours and attentions was always a source of surprise and speculation, especially since as a private person he was 'amiable, generous and charming, and infinitely patient with his students', to quote

Prof. Richard Silk, one of his most prominent former tutees and a life-long friend. Silk himself explained this aspect of his teacher's character with the fact that Simmons 'was a hard worker, who suffered immensely while working, and could not stand shallow admiration or hollow rhetoric for a moment without getting angry'. While passing into legend among literary scholars as a cantankerous hermit, Simmons nonetheless retained a select group of devoted friends who valued his personal qualities above his literary reputation.

Simmons, the great angry old man of Oxford, and perhaps one of the last true philosophers in Europe, died on 6 October 1989, aged 88. At his request, he was buried without ceremony in Oxford.

THE MANUSCRIPT AND ITS RECENT HISTORY

*

For some time Simmons was dismissed by colleagues as an 'old buffer' who had lost touch with the philosophical developments of his day. How far this judgement was from the truth is shown by his 'discovery' in America. Now that his philosophical insight and historical understanding have begun to be appreciated properly, it may be the proper moment to attempt an evaluation of his most puzzling legacy: the manuscript which was found among his papers in a red file which bears the crest of Oxford University and is marked *Recent Manuscripts & Drafts [The Editor]*. The manuscript, containing forty-five double-sided pages in Simmons' hand and some notes on separate sheets, is untitled and bears no explanatory remarks. One quotation, however, written on the inside flap of the file, seems to be very telling:

> fabulous incidents are as good as true ones, as long as they are feasible. Whether they happened or not, in Paris or in Rome, to John or to Peter, there is always some turn of the human mind about which they give useful information. I note and draw profit from these anecdotes, whether they are shadowy or substantial. Of the various readings that the histories often provide, I make use of the most unusual and memorable. There are some authors whose purpose it is to relate actual events. Mine, if I could fulfil it, would be to tell what might happen.
>
> (M. DE MONTAIGNE, On the Power of Imagination)

The manuscript itself is here presented in its original form and length, apart from eleven passages, which are literal transcriptions of passages of the *Oxford English Dictionary*, Volumes XI and XII, without any additions or omissions whatsoever, some of which extend over several pages. These have been omitted, as they cannot be considered as Simmons' original writing. The presence of these passages, however, does suggest that part of the extant manuscript was written on Simmons' 'black days', his depressive phases (for a closer psychopathological analysis see: 'Simmons' Writings in Analysis' by Alfred Wariacki, published in *Mind*, Sept. 1990, pp. 342–57). It is very difficult to assess when exactly it was written, but the suggestion by Prof. D. Trefusis of Fenland Polytechnic, based on evidence drawn from the development of Simmons' handwriting, that the period of its conception was probably between 1976 and 1983, is generally thought to be correct.

The manuscript was catalogued together with other of Simmons' papers, and it was only 'discovered' when these were despatched to the stacks of the library of Balliol College. Once the importance of the manuscript was realized, it was published almost immediately, and it sparked off a remarkable debate.

The discussion on the nature and intention of the manuscript is already so extensive that the different positions can be only hinted at here. There has been fierce discussion as to whether this account of a piece of extraordinary scholarship is fictional, or is an autobiographical representation of Simmons' work in the years 1976–9. While Huxley Mandel-brodt of Johns Hopkins University maintains that this is a subversive un-writing of the gender issue in European literature (a position elaborately argued in his article 'The Question of Femininity and the Demise of the Endangered Self in Simmons' Late Writings: a Deconstructionist Reading'), Alison Rover of Warwick University claims that it is nothing more than the diary of a project on which Simmons and some of his friends embarked in the summer of 1977, and which Simmons had to abandon because of mounting psychological difficulties. Another argument has been put forward by Prof. Silk of Oxford University. In a series of articles entitled *The Dramatic Persona of the Simmons Papers*, Silk has argued that the manuscript was based on the diaries of Simmons' father, who had a life-long passion for language, and who corresponded regularly with Sir James Murray, editor and founder of the *Oxford English Dictionary According to Historical Principles*. Other positions, suggesting that the work is a coded account of masonic rituals, a translation from ancient Hetitian hymns, or the manuscript of the long-lost novel *The Messiah* by Bruno Schulz, which Simmons acquired on a trip to the Ukraine in August 1967, and intended to publish under his own name, have failed to find a wide echo within the community of literary scholars.

Whether the manuscript published here is a work of art, the emanation of a surprisingly fruitful fantasy, a work of reminiscences, the document of the mental disarray and decay of a fine mind (thus G. Bloom), will be established through careful scholarship alone, and not by means of premature speculation. This edition does not therefore seek to provide a definitive version of the text in question, but merely an accessible and reliable source for research and information. For the convenience of the reader some footnotes have been added, clarifying certain points which might otherwise remain obscure to the general reader.

THE EDITOR
Oxford, July 12, 1993

THE MANUSCRIPT

FOUND AMONG THE POSSESSIONS

OF THE LATE

P. E. H. SIMMONS

Formerly Waynflete
Professor of Meta-
physical Philosophy at
Oxford University,
with an Introduction
and with Explanatory
Remarks, and for the
first time available to
the General Public in
this edition.

*

This little book is a concise summary of a nonexistent treatise, which its potential readers will in all probability be spared.

L. KOLAKOWSKI, 'The Presence of Myth', p. IX.

Personally I would much prefer not to appear in this ephemeral account of my work. The cause I serve, the undertaking I am devoted to, is much too grand, too important to be mixed up with the sphere of human destinies and fallacies, the fates of persons, their shortcomings, pettiness, futile aspirations and envy. However, it would be pointless to pretend that this report writes itself, and if you insist on calling me something, to pin a name to the author of this text in front of your eyes (I myself consider the obsession of the broader public with names and their connotations deplorable, even destructive), if you have to succumb to the urge of labelling the writer of these pages, who addresses you this very moment, you may think of me as P.[1]

---

1 The pseudonym 'P' has been the cause of much controversy. In the interpretation of Mandelbrodt and his followers, P designates 'paradigm', a notion which, in this reading, the text sets out to deconstruct by showing its inherent limitations and contradictions. 'The indefensible stronghold of the face of the dying Kronos falters from the owl, its death-ode on the phallus and His contemporaneous demise. The giant turns

This is not my name, nor is it because of any general prefer-
ence of this letter to others, nor an expression of some kind
of prejudice or by-belief; it just so happened that Dr Javis,
the editor-in-chief of this enormous project, has allocated
me the letter P as my domain.

Perhaps now, with this information at hand, it may dawn
on you what a gigantic responsibility rests on my shoulders
(which were never very strong). In the supreme effort of our
culture, the accumulation, compilation and editing of the
Definitive Dictionary of our language, it is subject to my
discretion, scholarship and meticulousness alone to discern
which word beginning with the letter P enters into the columns of the Dictionary, and thus into eternity. This means in
consequence that, when the edition is completed, should
that ever be the case, I must define which word may be
legitimately used and thought of, and which is to be
expelled. A word that has not been incorporated into
the Dictionary, says Javis, is no longer part of man-
kind.

---

back in agony and the very power against himself is the very
powerlessness against this power' (Mandelbrodt, *The Question of
Femininity*, pp. 345–6). According to this reading, the destruction of the
paradigm of male hierarchical order is what the text 'which is by no means
fiction, but an emanation of the act of writing in its existential peril itself'
(ibid.) sets out to prove. While A. Rover takes P as quite simply
Simmons' own initial, Richard Silk suggests that it stands for 'pater'.
'Simmons addressed his father with this name, traditionally used by
public school boys for "father", throughout his life until "pater" died in
1946' (*The Dramatic Persona*).

*

Probably it is an ironic coincidence that I was chosen for the letter P. You might have observed that there is a possibility of confusing me with the editor of certain passages of the Pentateuch, notably the book of Leviticus and the latter part of the book of Deuteronomy, who was baptized by scholars with this very name, to appear as this letter in journals of Biblical studies ever after, a solitary P as short form of 'priestly source', a name which serves to display how closely related my work is to his in subject and in significance. This is my ironical connection with the ancient P: he, a pre-historic editor, embarked on an important project; now I work on an important task bearing the same designation. I can, however, assure you that this identity in designation is merely incidental; incidental, but not without an inherent deeper meaning, for, where the P of old left off, founding our culture and by this act and in his writings laying dissent, controversy and misery at its very base, where he left off, the modern P, so to speak, which is my humble self, carries on. I am to conclude the chapter in our language, to erase controversy and disagreement, to settle all arguments and queries with authority. With an entry in the Dictionary all questions are settled, all uncertainties removed. The Dictionary will finally define our language beyond the level of ambiguity and doubt, and we will be able to start thinking clearly and to make ourselves understood unequivocally to everybody. My kingdom spans all words between P and pyxis (a capsular fruit which I myself have not yet been privileged to see). Within these borders I must deliver judgement and establish righteousness.

As warden of these areas of human life, of philosophy, pragmatism, poetry and pornography, poison, parrots, parodies, and purity, I am highly concerned, even shocked, at the level of irresponsibility on the part of certain individuals who shift the borders between letters, and consequently create havoc which may result in civil unrest and upheaval. (How can anybody talk if he is lost for words or they for him?) To my disgust, certain unhealthy trends have come to my notice which have already swamped other tongues and now endanger our idiom. The noble 'ph– ' , witness and certificate for a word's high breeding, has recently in some distasteful publications and even in artistic prose been substituted for a bland plebeian 'f– ' ! Were this disease to spread and finally become common usage before the First Edition, filosofy would be no longer in my department, exiled together with filology, fonology and so many others. This is what robs the world of all its certainty; words will, like Ahashver, wander through the labyrinths of modern usage, homeless and without orientation, and finally break down, tired from the endless journey, and pass away from our language.

How can a teacher guide a pupil to analyze phenomena, if he is not even sure how what he talks about is to be spelled, where it is to be found? Whether tomorrow it might not be fenomena, ffenomena or some other hideous corruption?

But more and even graver atrocities are committed against our language, in an attempt to assail its very core. So much do I loathe the very word that designates this abomination that I am eternally grateful that it is not within my department: neologism. Like venomous mushrooms, new words sprout from peoples' chaotic minds in an attempt at last to label what cannot be understood. Neologisms are the major enemy of our cause. How is the Dictionary to reach a state of perfection if new words keep pouring in from everywhere? One unsuspecting glance into any newspaper will demonstrate the scope of the disaster. Why, I keep asking myself, do people feel the sad urge to flood their troubled minds with ever new words, if they do not even know how to handle the richness of the existing corpus? Applications for the inclusion of new words are brought in by Malakh, the house messenger, every morning with the regular post, issues of different scholarly journals and the latest addition to the Communications. My policy, however, could not be more simple: as long as every existing word has not yet been fully expounded, taxed and exhausted in its meaning, so as to establish truthfully whether the existing language may indeed lack a certain shade of meaning, as long as this is not the case, no application can be considered, no suggestion can be taken seriously. The task of sorting out the valid from the spurious applications is most arduous and takes an intellectual audacity of the highest order. How is one to know whether some more obscure candidate, plwch, for example, or penanggalan, pinguefy, paraguathous, phyz, or piltock, to name a few, is a new coinage and to be expelled, or a time-honoured member of the assembly of words, whose fate it was to lead a marginal existence? Strenuous research is called for to ensure that only such words persist as are indeed entitled to have a place in the Dictionary. (As it happens, all the words quoted above have their place in the Dictionary.) In case of doubt, Malakh takes a new word to the office of Javis and there a committee meeting will be held with at least one member of the Great Academy, to which I myself am not admitted, and the answer comes within a day or so.

*

Practically unnoticed by the general public, whose attention is easily manipulated by a few journalists, the Dictionary has occupied the minds of some of the finest scholars in the country, some of whom are assembled in the publishing house. It was therefore much to my puzzlement and, I must admit, silent satisfaction, that an extensive article on the project of the Dictionary was recently published in one of our leading newspapers.[2] The subject, however, was not given its due prominence (the usual journalistic fascination

---

2 The fact that the article which is quoted here could not be traced in any
  major British newspaper between 1912 and 1946, the time covered by the
  diaries of Simmons senior, does seem to lend credibility to the theory that
  this text is indeed a work of fiction.

with meaningless detail got in the way), and it is possible that some readers may not have taken notice of the article at all. Allow me, therefore, to take the liberty of quoting a substantial part of the report again. The immediate subject of the article was, well, myself. I do not know why, of all editors, I was assigned the task of showing the gentleman from the press about the place and thus losing a valuable day's work. Surely there must have been a press officer in the house, but he may have been on holiday. Before commencing with the quotation I feel compelled to remark that I generally resent journalistic style and its careless and frivolous usage of words. In this instance especially I am forced to conclude that the article in no way gives an adequate impression of the intention underlying our work, or, for that matter, of my outward appearance. It is as follows:

I was met by the editor in the imposing marble entrance hall of the publishing house. I had arrived early and had already spent some ten minutes in the hall in front of the mighty curving staircase which leads up to the rooms where the offices of the editorial board and the office of the editor-in-chief are situated (as I came to learn later). The porter sat crouching in his lodge, a wooden compartment on the right of the two huge entrance doors. In appearance he was at least an octogenarian, shrunken into a gold-trimmed uniform which gave him the faded pomp of a field-marshal of some imperial army. Now the abundant decorations were dangling aimlessly from a chest that was no longer heroic but pneumonic, and the uniform itself was in aspect as careworn as his remaining fluff of yellowish hair. He seemed to conduct in his lodge a little business with pencils, paper and other bits and pieces, which were on display in one of the windows. One weak light bulb served to illuminate the compartment of this sad cerberus. When I asked him to inform my host of my arrival he gurgled something in a fragile tenor voice which made me think of a parrot sulking, and then despatched a message in a round box into the tube of what appeared to be the internal mail system. He then resumed his earlier posture and started with renewed energy to devote his attention solely to a sandwich which was lying in front of him on a bit of crumpled paper. Crumbs soon added to the decorations of his uniform, and after two futile attempts to draw the old man into conversation I left him to it and started looking around in the hall.

The building itself is apparently of imperial origin, with huge marble pillars supporting a plaster ceiling. I could not prevent a feeling of smallness and intimidation from creeping over me as I stood forlornly between the thick columns, and I felt how good it was that Samson had been blind when he tried to break the pillars of the Temple. Almost lost in these thoughts, I did not hear the arriving steps of a smallish man who now appeared at my side. He broke the hushed silence of the hall by asking whether it was me who awaited him, and after this was established muttered, 'Would you please follow me,' and, without paying any more attention to me, wandered off into the direction from which he had also presumably come. On our way I had ample opportunity to observe my strange host, if only from behind. He was of the tweedy type, though he now wore a grey suit. Beneath the grizzled hair I saw to my aston-ishment the gleam of a collar stud, the sort of thing which I had thought had been banished by now to the world of films and historical novels. Like an unexpected guest led by the butler through the recesses of an enormous and obscure country

house, I followed the little man through huge halls with tap-
estries and paintings depicting various saints and antique poets
in the act of writing, at times with little inspiring angels and
muses on their shoulders. We walked along seemingly endless
corridors, noble at first, then increasingly shabby and small,
down steps and stairs of creaking wood, until we finally
arrived in what seemed to be a cellar. Alongside the walls of
this subterranean gangway lay the tubes of the pneumatic
internal mail system, and every now and then a message whiz-
zed through one of the long winding iron snakes of pipeline
which stretched over the length of our way. On both sides long
rows of shelves packed with books and files lost themselves in
indeterminate darkness. Eventually we came to a door with the
letter P written prominently upon it. My host opened it and
showed me in. He switched on the light, a desk-lamp which
cast a bright light on a substantial volume lying on the table.

The whole room was covered with files, piling up to a threatening height along the walls, on shelves, on the floor, and
covering every bit of available space. A channel of free floor led
from the door to the desk and to the chair behind it. With
a pained expression my host removed a huge stack of files,
Privity–Probiscis, from the chair in front of the desk and asked
me to sit down. For a short time the pile, exceeding the size
of my host in height, seemed doubtful whether to rest in its
appointed place or to rain down in a cataract above the space
which it used to occupy, now taken by myself, but eventually it
seemed to decide to stay where it was. The desk-light cast
enormous shadows all over the walls, and the piles of paper
seemed transformed into huge, menacing sky-scrapers and
rocks, which towered blackly behind me.

My host began with a curious mixture of affability and curt-
ness: 'The Editor-in-chief, Dr Javis, decided to give me premises

where I could work in peace, undisturbed by sightseers, idlers or journalists. What you have just seen were the stacks. Every word which may be legitimately used in the future is stored there, catalogued, classified, and defined. This,' he said affectionately, and almost reverentially patting the huge volume in front of him, 'is the first draft of the section "P" of the Definitive Dictionary, which I have inherited from my predecessors. It has so far reached "patzer", but it is progressing rapidly, and I am already working on "petulance", "pew" and even "phaeton". Every new entry is written out in duplicate. One copy is glued into this volume, the other sent to the Editor-in-chief by pigeon post.' He chuckled. 'My colleague in "L" calls it "lifeline"; not that I ever see him, but gossip finds its way.' He became serious again. 'You must not think that we do all this merely to entertain ourselves. This is a serious undertaking, very serious indeed, hardly to be overestimated.' While my host went on to tell me about the wondrous significance of his work, I took the opportunity of having a good look at him I now faced for the first time since I had walked behind him on the way to the office. He was a small and stout man, perhaps fifty years of age. The three-piece suit he wore cannot have been fashionable at any time, but might perhaps have been considered a classic thirty years ago. His face was difficult to describe, since it could have belonged to any man of his age: small bags underneath the watery eyes, a nose which was not prominent but had hair growing out of it, a high forehead, and greyish hair, assembled in a respectful circle around a prominent bald patch. The fact that he was indeed wearing a wing collar which was no longer quite white and which stood rigidly in sharp contrast to the soft folds of his neck, gave him the impression of being not in a real-life situation, but in a grotesque novel. What exactly his work was, who paid him, and when the publication of the Dictionary is envisaged, I was unable to ascertain. His descriptions were so full-mouthed and grand, that under close scrutiny they seemed to disintegrate altogether . . .

Pardon my malignancy, but I cannot but feel quiet satisfaction (again) at the reaction of the journalist, except for the fact that his description of my person, reproduced here only for the sake of honesty, is untrue, and indeed makes me seem more like the invention of a youthful writer than a real person; but this is journalism, my suspicions of which I always find justified.

At this point the reader, expecting an account of my work, its object, and its hidden traps and difficulties (for this is what this account is really concerned with), is asked to bear with me while I make a slight deviation into the realm of the personal. It is not at all my habit to bother the reader with musings about myself, and certainly excursions like this will not in any way become the object of these meditations, but I do feel that I have to correct an impression which might have been given to those reading the article quoted above. Of course I do not have my office in a dark hole in the cellar, surrounded by piles of paper and ghostly shadows on the walls. My office is a well-sized room with a window into the courtyard in the main building, floor three, room B 304.[3] I felt, however, that it is hardly fair to lead

---

3 This location has not been decoded by literary scholars. To his puzzlement, however, the editor of these pages has realized that it corresponds with his own room in his college.

someone who is in pursuit of sensational news alone into the realm of hard and often boring facts. It would not satisfy his appetite for the extraordinary and thus would lead him to invent things and to distort reality in the same way as he distorted my appearance for the sake of a few clever formulations (my collar, which it is only correct to wear in keeping with the solemnity of the work at hand, contrasting with the 'folds of my neck'! I *ask* you!). I wanted to prevent the good man, who after all is merely pursuing his sad profession, from being tempted to misrepresent a reality which *prima facie* is indeed completely ordinary and does not excite comment.[4] This is why I led him to the storeroom in the cellar-stacks, where the files for P are kept, waiting to be worked on – a far more picturesque spot than my office, if a little less comfortable. He was impressed, which was what he had come for, thus both parties were served to full satisfaction. The work we do here is far too important to be distorted by any journalistic taste for the freakish in this world. The representation of myself shows how little interest in truth he really had. He was out for a story, and a story he got.

---

4 Mandelbrodt writes about this section: 'The existential horror about the dark abyss of irony *beyond* the playful reserve of the author's narcissistic self-image confronts him with his own creation, the head of Medusa, and forces him into the pose of the manipulative father-god by inversion of the casuistry of the aetiology of anxiety.'

*

Perhaps this is the time to introduce you to the workings of this office. Every day Malakh, the inter-office messenger, comes in with new files, requested books, the mail and newly arrived scholarly journals. Almost every time a supplement to the Communications of the Great Academy is part of the pile of things which Malakh brings me. The Communications are of crucial importance to my work and I will have to tell you about them in detail some other time. Malakh, whose name suggests that he is a stranger to this country, and probably of Slavonic extraction, is my link with the higher realms of the publishing house, notably with the office of Dr Javis, Editor-in-chief of the Definitive Dictionary. Javis is indeed so far removed from the sphere of ordinary office work and editing that I myself have not yet had the privilege of meeting him, or of being summoned to his office, although this is undoubtedly bound to happen at some point in the future. There is some dispute among the sub-editors and office clerks whether Dr Javis handles notes and queries addressed to him directly, or whether this is the work of his personal secretary, Mr Lloyd. From a strictly rational point of view there is little evidence that Lloyd intercedes at all. I myself would go even further in considering Lloyd entirely fictitious, one of those myths which arise during such a complex undertaking as the editing of the Definitive Dictionary over a long time when communication is poor. The stories about Lloyd are more irritating than anything else, and some of them positively offend my aesthetic sensibilities, for instance the fact that he is said to go about in sandals, footwear most inappropriate for anyone in his position. The invention of a personal secretary may also be attributed to the fact that Javis works in complete segregation from the staff. It may be a consolation for weaker natures to know that not everything depends on the inaccessible Javis in his office alone. I myself am completely content with doing my work as it is, and follow the directions set out by his office without the rather self-important aspiration of getting personally into contact with Javis; Malakh after all will deliver queries in writing, although this is a procedure which I am extremely reluctant to follow, on the assumption that Javis is a very busy man. Still, it is sometimes consoling to know that, theoretically, the possibility of direct communication does exist.

*

P as a letter is a vast mystery.

I felt deeply honoured that Dr Javis deemed me fit for this gigantic task. Not only is it the third-biggest letter in the alphabet, closely following S and C, but it is shrouded in riddles and mysteries. Its origin is clear and its noble pedigree can be traced back to the oldest Semitic tongues. It used to be the fifteenth letter of the Phoenician alphabet, written ٦ or ٢, and was taken over by the Hebrews, who have preserved it to this day as ٦. To us it was brought by the Greeks, who adopted it (like most other letters) and changed its direction, and then its form to π. The Romans finally gave us our P, and only later did it suffer a dislocation from its rightful place to number sixteen by the introduction of J into the alphabet as a proper letter.

It is not this that makes it mysterious, nor indeed is it the linguistic aspect (except for the remarkable fact that, alone among the Indo-Europeans, the Celts and Armenians seemed to dislike it and hardly used it at all). P was a small and modest letter in early modern times, but a flood of Oriental, Latin, French, and even African words then boosted its size, and left behind a host of words pregnant with etymological riddles and uncertainties. It is a letter of immigrants; the loving and attentive ear hears the buzzing of a hundred foreign tongues within it: hymns of the early church; the babble and yelling of Arabian bazaars; Latin precision, elegance and brutality; Germanic harshness; words sailing with William the Conqueror; words drowned with the Spanish Armada (some of which mysteriously drifted ashore); Arabic prose and philosophy; commands given by Hadrian; and psalms, all humming, bubbling and chattering, colourful and delightful.

This now may make you understand how humbling my task is: to discipline the multitude, to order all these disparate elements according to the most natural method. To complete this task may take many generations.

*

Prolific minds have worked before me on issues of lexicography without solving the riddle of how to find the perfect, the definitive method of writing a dictionary. Potocki[5] and Humbold,[6] Duden,[7] and Sir James Murray[8] have all spent great parts of their lives trying to find adequate ways of describing, defining and moulding a language so far that it was indeed captured in the pages of their works. Even in this place I am not the first to undertake this work. The man who occupied my chair before myself is incidentally not totally unknown to me, since I inherited, after his sudden and tragic death, not only his notes and drafts for hundreds of words, but also many of his personal belongings. According to Malakh the poor man died of a heart attack when he found one of his research results contradicted by Javis himself, an occurrence of the utmost rarity. The whole course of events is most pitiable, and indeed mysterious. It was concerning the origin of the word 'parley' that events took their fatal course. My predecessor had duly established that this word, stemming from the French 'parlée', was first used by Standyhurst in his *Ænaïs* in 1582, where the sentence 'Her bye tale owt hauk-

5 Jan Potocki (1761–1815), writer, scholar and politician.
6 Wilhelm von Humbold (1765–1835), literary scholar and grammarian, brother of Alexander von Humbold.
7 Konrad Duden (1829–1911), German lexicographer.
8 Sir James Henry Murray (1837–1915), British lexicographer.

ing amyd of her parlye she choketh,' is to be found. The Editor-in-chief, however, accused him in an editorial note of forgetting the usage of this word in Carlyle's *Treatise on the True Easie Parlance or Eloquencia* from 1578, and quoted its sentence 'With Lords and Gentlemen canst not thou parlye but an thou knowest rhetoricke.' The poor man is said to have collapsed on the spot as if struck by lightning as soon as he had read the communication, before the eyes of Malakh, who was, however, unable to help him. The mistake which had caused him to die of shame seems all the more surprising, since the work which he left behind him was of outstanding solidity and scholarship. My own research into the reference given by the high office had disturbing results, since I was unable to verify it; the book was nowhere to be found. Perhaps it belongs to Javis' private collection. The fact remains that even Carlyle, the author of the quotation, seems to be so obscure that he has escaped Renaissance scholarship altogether.[9]

The erudition and work of my predecessor meant that I could sometimes directly carry on where the pen, so to speak, had fallen from his hand. Now, on several files his majestic calligraphic capitals and underscores, testifying to his solid education, stand next to my own thinner and more

---

9 The author here seems to be confused, or to confuse his reader wilfully. For a detailed biography of Hugh Carlyle, one of the great writers of odes and orations in the 1570s, see *The Exact Muse, Carlyle and the Elizabethan Ode* by H. Trasher (Cambridge, 1975).

erratic hand. Indeed, 'parleye' to 'parmeliaceous' may be considered a joint effort. I find his work most satisfying, though of course my judgement is open to question. Besides, it is a part of human nature to be afflicted with the curse of having to make mistakes; even the most able will stumble sometime.

Apart from the usual office implements, a few remarkable objects which used to belong to my predecessor remain in my possession. A silver-framed picture, showing a group of children, perhaps his, a short and strongly bent pipe, still half-filled with tobacco, and an old-fashioned knife, the kind used to sharpen writing utensils. He seems on the whole to have been a rather quiet and placid gentleman, with no ambition to excel beyond his appointed place. I have lately taken to using his pipe, a most pleasant occupation, although it almost drives me underground on account of certain groups of confused and misled individuals who claim that, by doing so, I am damaging not only my health and thus the national economy, but also, with the smoke, our whole milieu (what utter rot!).

Silent and domestic as he was, my predecessor had one all-devouring passion, which he followed with considerable singlemindedness: he had an extraordinary fondness for plants. On my first day in office, flowers and shrubs of all sorts and extractions crowded the room, standing upon the desk, the floor, the window-sill, dangling in great pots from the ceiling, swimming in the sink and distributed as seedlings in little cups on the desk. Malakh told me the man was totally devoted to his collection and spent hours cutting, watering, spraying, counting buds, and the like pursuits. To me as a horticultural layman, some of the plants seemed to be very eccentric choices indeed: in a big pot a pine tree, to my knowledge not a typical office plant, led a miserable and prickly existence; primroses, albeit out of season, blossomed on the window-sill with cheerful radiance; next to them a patch of parsley looked dull and somewhat lost. Overshadowed by a palm of sorts, a couple of poppies shone with almost aggressive redness, filling the whole room with a smell so irritating that I asked Malakh to get rid of them as soon as possible, together with the pondweed which had its place in a considerable pool in the sink, and the seedlings which took up most of the space on the desk. As I am truly not a specialist in plants it is not possible for me to recall all their names, but it hardly matters now, since fortunately most of them are gone. Only some primroses, part of what used to be a huge colony, still hold a modest place on the window-sill, showing with all due discretion that this room has a history which extends beyond my own work. If the obsession with plants of all kinds was a slightly eccentric trait, I am deeply indebted to the gentleman for something else. Among the possessions which he involuntarily left to me, the deceased had counted a little notebook, which I found in the uppermost drawer, together with a box of dry tobacco, an apple, half-eaten, and some other miscellanea. It was a little notebook, which appeared to be a scholarly diary or journal, in which a method of lexicography was established without which, in my view, the section 'P' in the Dictionary could never be complete. An artistic technique emerged from these pages, capable of redressing the sometimes painfully disturbed balance of language. The scope of this idea, which has become crucially important to my own thinking, extends far beyond the realm of mere deductive scholarship and endorses a wider argument, perhaps even bordering on the mystical. According to the theory put forward in the notebook, throughout the evolution of language, some words out of the pool of possibilities, meanings, nuances and significances have flourished into the form and strength we know today, while others have been condemned to lead a marginal existence, stagnant and fragmented, used, if at all, only by imbeciles, prophets, wise men and babes. They escaped the net of scholarly recognition and finally their usage ceased altogether. Atrophied, shrunken into their embryonic stage and totally neglected, these words still exist in hiding, like the larvae of a butterfly under a coat of snow, only to come out again when they are called upon. The attentive reader will in such a case notice a gap between two words, a missing sound, or concept, which he then must restore with the sensitivity of the true artist, or, as the notebook puts it with exquisite taste, 'return to language its prodigal sons'. The notebook, after having established this fact, goes on to state that the really observant editor who strives to write a truly comprehensive dictionary must trace these words and reinstate them at least as possibilities. These words are not neologisms, far from it!

Where the latter is the crude invention of a new word out of ignorance of the abundance provided by language already, the task of restoration is only to reinstate what has existed all along.

The art developed in the notebook may be obscure, practised only by the fewest people, now perhaps only by myself. I would not be surprised if this were so, though it would make my responsibility all the greater. Some kindred spirits in the world of poetry, into which I often delve, both for pleasure and for duty, follow the principle of restoration with wonderful sense and sensitivity; while some thrash about in utter ignorance.

A random example: between 'penumbrous' and 'penur' the trained and perceptive mind senses a gap that cannot be filled without imagination. The symmetry of the whole page may be at risk, the balance of a tongue unhinged, just because nobody has seen that 'penupy' is the obvious and necessary word that alone can fill the awesome abyss. As to the meaning of such a regained word, this is a matter of wholly secondary interest. It will be discovered, rediscovered, just like its mortal coil, the word itself. This example was taken from the notebook, but I myself have been able to supply some additions and completions of my own: 'piebent' (between 'piebald' and 'piece') and, daring but absolutely necessary and entirely adequate, 'pilbout' (between 'pilaw' and 'pilch', a great step which had to be taken).

I admit that this art must seem somewhat mysterious,

even obscure, to the untrained eye, but as in every refined pursuit in human life, the mind must be attuned to the novelties and joys of any idiom. If my immediate predecessor was a poet and a visionary as well as a scholar, the man who was in charge of P before him was an exact opposite. (I happen to know these facts because of the reports of good old Malakh, who seems to have served in his present capacity for as long as human memory recalls, at least for as long as the porter can remember, and he recently celebrated his ninety-third birthday. The porter took on his work, which he inherited from his father, when he was fourteen, first as an under-porter and message-boy, then, after his father met his sad death when he found himself confronted head-on with one of the first automobiles, he succeeded him, and took up the position which he was to hold ever since. I presume, by the way, that his uniform is inherited from his grandfather, who, as the porter once told me, full of pride, fought at Waterloo and was patted on the head by Wellington himself. For as long as the porter can remember, Malakh has been there, seemingly ageless, though already no longer young. Malakh occasionally speaks about the history of the publishing house, and the changes and traditions which it has seen.)

As Malakh relates, the editor before the visionary poet was a dull, uninspired worker, for whom the task eventually proved too much, so that he found himself forced to take refuge in mysticism and occult speculations.

After studying at some continental university he wrote a

dissertation on a grammatical theme (the subjective prefix past participle in the middle high German court poetry of Burgundy and the Rhineland, if Malakh remembers correctly). Malakh told me all this when I once invited him for tea in my room. I have an electric kettle in my room, which is lodged underneath the sink. It would not be an exaggeration to call this my only convenience here, the fountain of life and comfort in my long hours of research and patient work. It is an ordinary metal kettle (made by Russell Hobbs) with a black handle and a white switch, which, when filled with two cups of cold water from the tap above, goes 'click' exactly one and a half minutes after having been switched on. I usually take Earl Grey in little paper sachets, bought in packs of fifties in the little shop on the way to the café in which I take my lunch. The sound of the water bubbling excitedly against the walls of the kettle is the most consoling thing imaginable. Malakh was the only one whom I ever invited to tea, indeed, the only one ever to enter the room apart from myself, at least during working hours. In his wondrous and long-winded way Malakh told me about the Doctor, as my predecessor's predecessor preferred to be addressed, and about his fate. One day I was busy preparing a cup for myself, when Malakh came with the daily delivery. I invited him to have a cup together with me, and he accepted sheepishly, taking a seat in front of my desk, like a solicitor's client. It took a good deal of asking and encouragement to extract from him the fortunes of the office and its occupants. With circumloquations and courteous expressions he successfully navigated around any direct description of the Doctor and his fate. Stripped from its corset of courtesy and old world politeness, the account of the scholar in question is as follows. The Doctor led the life of a hermit and seldom left the room; indeed, the cleaners had suspected that he even slept there. He always wore plain dark clothes and would flash mistrusting looks at everybody from over his pince-nez (the Doctor looked at everybody with the utmost attention, as Malakh put it). His beliefs, which he did not hesitate to make known, were, as Malakh relates, 'of some uncommon and intriguing persuasion'; as I take it he was a member or founder of a nature-loving sect, strictly vegetarian and a firm believer in weak herbal teas, of which he took several every day in a prescribed order linked to the constellation of the planets. The work of his which has come to my eyes confirms my suspicion of his unhealthy eccentricity. Completely lost in details, his main occupation, as far as editorial work is concerned, seems to have been counting the occurrences and variations of a particular word since it was first used, and analyzing the deviations of its standard spelling according to a self-devised system. His single-minded interest in linguistic fineries seems to have been compensated for rather heavily by his interest in mysticism, and eventually, after several minutes of embarrassed evasions, Malakh confided that the Doctor came to neglect his duties and wrote a weighty tome of theosophical content, in which he revealed himself as the reincarnation of the Boddhisatva.

Out of a mixture of plain curiosity and the faint hope of perhaps finding another nugget of insight into lexicography, I asked Malakh to provide the book for me, and he did so on the next day, making me sign a copy of Declaration 14b of the internal library (concerning the handling of documents of obscure, subversive or pornographic nature, and of aggressively nonsensical documents) for the head librarian. In this declaration, I had to vow not to give any of the information obtained to those under eighteen, anyone generally understood to be morally weak or with leanings towards the philosophy of mind. The book was bound in purple linen, on which a nebulous figure was drawn in fine gold, and around it the title *Insights into the Lucidity of the Occult and the Mysterium of the Divine Letter*. On the frontispiece there was a photograph of a man looking into the camera over a pair of tiny glasses with an air of mild disgust. His black hair was firmly brilliantined backwards and he wore, not to my knowledge after the fashion of his time, a large black ribbon made of atlas silk instead of a tie. His whole appearance was, if I may make a personal comment, something between a shaven Rasputin and an archduke who, because of his excessive eccentricities, is prudently kept by his relatives in the ancestral castle. In the work itself, written to my irritation with the air of one who tells a truth which only an imbecile or a malignant philistine could fail to see, the Doctor set out on the road to salvation. Man, he wrote, had fallen out with divine wisdom, because he had yielded to the temptation to use language for the realm of the profane and entertaining. Language, once the property of only a chosen and initiated few, had been betrayed and vulgarized beyond repair. Salvation lay for man, the Doctor explained with the attitude of a professor teaching a demented toddler (I beg you to forgive my polemic outbursts, which betray my irritation), in meditation in order to attain the spiritual discipline necessary to re-attune himself to the divine wisdom, which would then pour out the Grace now withheld from man. I was surprised to find Lloyd, the alleged secretary of Dr Javis, mentioned here as one of the great leaders of spiritual life. My discomfort with the whole book surmounted my scholarly patience, albeit well trained by hundreds of hours of desperate boredom and suppressed anger about the shallowness of most arguments put forward in print, and I closed the book at the beginning of the section in which the Doctor promised to explain a few 'basic exercises' for the pursuit of spirituality with the feeling of having made a narrow escape.

The Doctor's fate was linked with his magnum opus. In Chapter VII (where else?) he explained that it was his mission on earth to rebuild the salomonic temple, the true measurements of which the Grace had revealed to him. In an architectural drawing in his own hand, the temple appeared to have the shape of a gigantic P.

Javis, on being told of the exploits of one of his staff, immediately sent down Malakh with an editorial note, stating that he required the Doctor's services no longer. The Doctor, who took this as confirmation of a satanic conspiracy against him, but more likely out of hurt pride, hanged himself three days later.

*

Perhaps it has not escaped your notice that my two predecessors were individuals inclined to mystical speculations. Whether this was personal disposition and therefore to a degree natural and unavoidable, or whether the specific nature of the work made them so inclined, I dare not say. As for myself I do not share any such speculative preferences. True, I indulge in the same art as the editor before me who invented it, resurrecting lost words, but this is merely a sensitization to the obvious, the process of learning to listen to words and voices which emanate from files. It is in no way a mystical speculation which strives to combine the compellingly obscure with the absurd, and which substitutes feelings and profound half-truths for even a shadow of real knowledge. I do not lose myself and my work in personal feelings, and indeed I have always maintained that it is strictly necessary to maintain a firm division between the professional and the private. I can assure you, and you undoubtedly will be relieved to learn this, that 'P' as a letter or as a principle has in no way invaded my life, which is perfectly ordinary, that neither my living place nor anything else was chosen to harmonize with my profession by commencing with this letter.

I do not intend to bore you with accounts of my own life,

because for the present purpose, indeed in most respects, it is entirely irrelevant. The work at hand, the fascination to which others have so tragically succumbed, is so vast that it alone provides more than enough material for my testimony. I, on the other hand, middle-sized in every respect, can hardly expect you to be interested in a life which in no way exceeds the ways of the everyday and ordinary. If you want to know me (I do not see why, but stranger things have happened), look at my colleagues in publishing houses, at people on the street, their little needs, predilections and unaccountable small idiosyncrasies and perversities; no point adding to the list by recounting yet another instance. To drive home the argument, allow me to tell you this. My workplace in no way offers anything beyond the ordinary. (It is often advisable, perhaps even life-saving, to cling to the ordinary, the perfectly normal, if the task at hand is so fantastic and in many ways not free from the danger of mystical speculation. Only by means of this is it possible to retain a firm footing in reality, and sharpening a pencil is often in the course of the day the only method of returning to the framework of the real, so as not to be transported away into some unknown region by the sheer delight of discovery or the ecstasy of sounds, colours and meanings. This increases my consumption of pencils considerably, and there have been some instants when I have been forced to spend hours in sharpening pencils until there was nothing left to sharpen and I had to ring Malakh for a fresh supply, but it has been proven to be an effective method of maintaining sanity. I do possess one of those practical pencil-sharpeners which are firmly installed on the edge of the table, and which thus becomes in more than one respect a symbolic anchor to the world of fixed facts. It is a constant joy to use it, to insert a pencil into the iron fangs which close like the eye of a photographic camera, and then slowly to turn the handle round and round again, and to see the pencil gradually decreasing in length.)

My desk is one of those work-places which were covered a long time ago with leather, which by now has disintegrated into a wooden sea with tiny little leather islands, a map of some unknown archipelago in the south seas. Much of the far side is covered with water stains, a reminder of the obsession of my predecessor, but most of them are now invisible, covered by files and journals, some volume of the Communications or other documents of a related kind. Indeed, the only space remaining free is directly in front of me and just about big enough to host my elbows and one opened file. While on the right the pencil-sharpener clutches the edge of the table like a plump parrot, to my left and within easy reach is the tea-cup, an old family piece and the only piece of sentimental value that I allow myself in this room (not one of those hideous office mugs with the owner's name, cartoon figures or other abominations all over them).

In order to write an entry in a file, inkpots are still used in this house, and a strangely but dearly and familiarly shaped pot of Waterman ink (*noir*)[10] is standing right in front of me. The pens and pencils all stand upright in a glass container (formerly a humble water-glass), all crowded together – the proletariat, tools for notices and margins, easily erasable with a rubber – together with the proud and long-stretched ink pens, whose writings are invariably for eternity.

I must confess that in a sense even I am a victim of this daunting work. Invariably the study of words, their history, meaning and evolution, etymology, connotations and for-mation, must impress on any mind its seal, especially since some words will resound for a certain person more than others and come to exercise a considerable influence of their own on any mind connected with them. This long-winded proëm which I am engaging in now seems necessary before I can tell what I hardly dare admit: that I am subject to daydreams, voices and visions. Words, p-words, emit and emanate images, stories, pictures and fantasies, which ulti-mately are impossible to keep at bay. Research supplies a multitude of fascinating facts and figures, and sometimes they tend to take on a life of their own, an existence inde-pendent of the written letter from which they wax. They start to hover and flow in one form or the other, kaleido-scopes of phantasm and meaning, in shapes and appear-ance rich and strange. This reason alone drove me to sit down and write this account of my work and all facts close

10 Mandelbrodt: 'The cultural effort writes itself in the blackness of its impending doom.' (*pace* Mandelbrodt!)

to it, as an analysis, which, in re-reading, might supply my often tortured brain with some clue, some unnoticed detail, which might help me to ban those apparitions and their unhealthy consequences. I must repeat: I categorically refuse to feature as the main character of this narration, as it is a position which I am neither fit nor willing to occupy; the oscillating images alone which at times occupy my mind, the work itself and its manifold fascinations, these are the things which have informed my need to write these pages. I only want to write them down, to fix them once and for all and banish them from ruling over my mind and innermost feelings. On paper, transfixed into a network of black lines and curves, paralyzed by my own writing hand, they are no longer alive and dangerous, but merely objects, which now adhere to my terms, liable to be read, re-read, laid aside, scraped out, burned, folded into a glider, thrown away or even printed. They are my royal subjects as soon as I have drawn them into my realm, where I can edit them, pronounce upon them, even forget them. Were I to let these apparitions have the upper hand and throw my mind into the most unworldly torments, states and convulsions, I fear my inner disposition might one unhappy day no longer be able to recover and remain petrified for the remainder of its existence plunged into an abyss of voices and hallucinations. It is madness that my predecessors could not withstand (and the cataloguing of P is still only at its very beginnings, partly for reasons which I will come to explain) and which I try to foil by distilling the whirlwind of haunted images and all too idyllic revelry into the bluntness and uncompromising clarity of the written word. I am a mineworker of language, I inhale centuries of ambiguities and meanings like coal dust. If I do not attempt to cast all this into a definite shape I would slowly dissolve, disintegrate (like others before me) into a mere cloud of possible editors, meanings and spellings: editor, edeetur, edditer, adittur, aditur, edcitur, etceter, etc, etc.

No word is innocent. Words are obsessed and haunted spirits. Once unchained from their heavy bond of syntax and strict grammaticality, they can do anything, start to dance, whirl and revolve, like a bunch of mad little devils. As in a cave, it is impossible to move without provoking a host of echoes, resounding mockery, threatening grumbles and reverberations. No word can be used without silliness and indecency, the pure word is defiled by its very existence amongst others; even quotations from the classical texts drown in a flood of babbling and yelling voices:

> – BLESSED ARE THE POOR IN SPIRIT,
> FOR THEIRS IS THE KINGDOM OF HEAVEN.

– He is poor whom God hateth!
– Crist with his apostils lyvede most povere lif . . .
– O poor Anathoth!
– Poor men have no souls!
– . . . of poor but honest parents . . .
– Goddamn the poor!!

– Pour moi?

– Blissed be thai that er pover in spirit!

– Poor old stinker, dead and gone, his face you'll see no more!

– Blissed be thai . . .

– Poor little rich girl, you're a bewitched girl! better beware!

– Blissed be . . .

– *Shut up!!*

– It is a poor soul that never gives nature a fillip!

– Poor as a coot!

– He is not poor that desireth little!

– He seems altogether a poor and debile being.

– 'Ees a poor man, ee gôôs to work.

– Thy poor brother.

– Poor job, wadn't it sir?

– Blessed is he that considereth the poor and needy.

– A poor beauty finds more lovers than husbands.

– Lest the poor man come!

– Puyr boddeis . . .

– Bodies!

– . . . and forget not the congregation of the poor!

AMEN

*

Perverted and confused as is our whole vocabulary, our every means of expression, we are in sore need of a definitive, the Definitive Dictionary, which once and for all defines every word according to its nature and leaves no doubt about it whatsoever. We have to help the words to struggle from an inferno of polluted meanings, to bring them back to their original beauty and creative force. If the only realm of clarity in language is to be found in empirical science, we will be choked by reviews of our life, criticism thereof, scholarly remarks about it, definitions and contradictions of it, theories, statistics and demographies. Talking about life will swamp life itself and make it superfluous. Life will be something described, never experienced. This is why our task is a great one. The method of this compilation, the Dictionary, is essential. Perhaps tracing back every word down to the very first usage, omitting no single instance in which it was ever used, may force it to reveal itself. Unfortunately, such a work could never be written, printed or read without contradicting its aim. It would be a tombstone, not a remedy.

*

Practically every aspect of the editorial work is governed by the regulations which come to my office in the supplements to the Communications of the Great Academy. The Great Academy was set up quite some time ago by Dr Javis for the purpose of discussing and regulating the method in which the editing of the Definitive Dictionary is to be conducted.

The Communications of the Great Academy are issued in daily supplements which are then collected in mighty tomes for the purposes of reference and study by all editors. Since our work is of profound, not to say universal importance, it should not be surprising that every conceivable aspect of it has been, and still is regulated by the Great Academy. Its members are the most esteemed scholars in the field, highly respected in the community of the learned. The rulings laid down in the Communications are mostly considered to be inspired by Dr Javis, who indeed is often quoted in the work. The rulings encompass every possibility, provide for all contingencies. From the consumption of sandwiches during working hours to the format of the writing paper, the standardized way of using paper clips, the size of handwriting required, institutional anecdotes, observance of working hours, the breeding of cacti and herbs by the window, appropriate dress (wing collar, naturally), opportunities for washing hands, the recitation of poems for various occasions, ethical observations, dress for formal occasions (not that I have had the privilege of witnessing any, but gowns must be worn), personal feuds between Academy members, legal aspects, nothing escapes their attention, everything is endowed with at least two conclusive and often conflicting opinions and rulings on the matter. At times hints are even made concerning the nature of editing. You may demand a sample, an impression of what this compendium is like; however, I am decidedly reluctant to quote from it *in extenso*, not for the fear of giving anything away, but simply because it requires considerable training to be able to appreciate the depth and wisdom of this book, an ability to read between the lines without which the student of the Communications may find himself perplexed or even irritated, since the way in which the points are made may be somewhat unusual to the modern reader. Still, I have expressly set out to explain my work, and, as this is an important part of the work, I will have to relate it as well. Allow me therefore to quote a random example from the Communications and to annotate it for your greater convenience in the customary way of the tomes of commentary and analysis which are published on issues discussed in the Communications. The style, which some readers may find somewhat cryptic, is merely resting on a scholarly convention and is, let me assure you, to the adept no more enigmatic than an article in a newspaper. The scientific jargon employed, largely obsolete by now as far as wider knowledge is concerned, is in fact very precise, elegant and effective. The sheer comprehensiveness and the already substantial number of volumes have further necessitated a certain density of style which needs to be enlarged upon by the understanding reader. This makes it a true companion for consultation and edification in all cir-cumstances; whatever the question, there is the certainty that a couple of answers can always be found. Let me now show you one of these pages, chosen merely because it hap-pened to lie open on my desk, since I stopped my reading from the previous evening at that point. The passage (Folio

103a) deals with the creation of new words, a matter close to my heart. As promised I have supplied some explaining notes.[11]

WHOSOEVER WRITES A NEOLOGISM, WHETHER WITH HIS RIGHT OR LEFT, THE SAME OR DIFFERENT, EVEN WITH TWO DIFFERENT INKS, IN ANY TONGUE, IS GUILTY. PROF. JOYCE[12] SAID: THE WRITING OF TWO LETTERS IS PROHIBITED BECAUSE OF THE MARKING OF THINGS. PROF. YOUNG SAID: SMALL NAMES CAN BE PARTS OF BIGGER NAMES, BE FOR BEEHIVE, GO FOR LOGOS ETC.

It is clear that one is guilty if one writes with the right, for it is the way of writing, but why with the left, for this is not the way? Prof. Jameson suggested: this is taught because of lefthanders. – But then with him it should be the left as with the others the right, for this is the way of writing! However, Prof. Abbey has related a tale about someone who could use both his hands. Prof. Arnold, the

---

11 The intention behind this cryptic text is unclear, and consequentially interpretations abound. Mandelbrodt sees in it 'the archetypal un-ravelling of a text, conquering the complacency of meaning with repetition and explanation as dialectical poses of the lyrical self'. A. Wariacki detects in this passage the first symptoms of manifest psycho-pathological disorder, quite in conflict with A. Rover, who reads the passage as the 'escapades of an old man who has set out to fool the critics'. The reader is advised to find his own interpretation.

12 The usage of the name Joyce in this context has been interpreted as an attempt by Simmons to throw light on some of the darker passages of *Finnegans Wake* in this exegetical part of the text.

son of the notorious Mr. Arnold, said, this is the opinion of Prof. Joyce, who claims that writing and marking an object amounts to the same. − But if we adopt the conclusion of Prof. Joyce, then we cannot agree with Joyce from the start! − It is all after Joyce. [etc., etc., etc.]

Whosoever: whichever editor includes such an abomination in his work and thereby makes it official usage. This is the explanation of Prof. Bomberg, but Prof. Meier holds that it refers to any person using language. *a neologism*: a word which does not take its authority from informed restoration, but from wild and haphazard guessing. *right or left*: with either hand, another authority in the field claims in the name of Prof. Handstreich that it is meant to be 'right and left', i.e. using a typewriter or keyboard instead of writing by hand. *the same or different*: the same letters. It does not matter in the least what the form of the new word is. *event*: should be understood also in the biblical sense: especially if someone tries to dissociate himself from writing something like a neologism in any of his files by writing a part in pencil, and thus passing it off as an accidental note. *inks*: different colours, to lend the word, which is still white and unused, some colour, at least externally, with the hope that it might take it on. *in any tongue*: even if the word is seemingly nonsensical there will be a language in which the word could mean something. *is guilty*: of betraying the effort of the Dictionary and thus liable to be made redundant. *writing of two letters*: only two letters in combination can be seen as a new word. *the marking of objects*: here Joyce is clearly taking issue with Saussure, because the claim is that objects, in a metaphysical sense, have to be marked, designated appropriately, and not just with arbitrary sign structures. *small names*: read: words. *bigger names*: it is likewise illicit to stick together several already established words as particles of another word.

This short passage may serve to illustrate the problems met by anyone who searches for the correct procedure and method. The problematic feature of the Communications is that the Professors are so immersed in a heated discussion that they never actually have time to edit their finds, and so the individual scholar has to plough his way through the protocols of the meetings (all my admiration goes out to the man writing the protocol, who even has spare time to include private gossip), without being introduced either to the motion debated, or the outcome of the debate the next day. Fortunately, there is an extensive body of commentaries and explanations (admittedly some of them are considerably less lucid than the discussions concerned). The structure of the discussion emerges with experience, as does the delight of understanding, for instance when the reader discovers the controversies between the schools of thought of Hill and Shambles, which go on throughout all the discussions.

*

Patience and passion are the core of my work.

Every morning at 7.55 I walk into the vast building of the publishing house and briefly nod to the porter on my right. Every morning he extends his head out of his withered uniform, from the recesses of his high collar, like an old turtle, and gives me a look of puzzled apprehension. Every morning I take the rattling lift up to the third floor, hoping that it will not give up its feeble ghost with this latest strain on its structure. Every morning I utter a sigh of relief when I find myself safely delivered to the third floor, and make headway to my office.

In my room I struggle out of my coat, something I have never learned to do with elegance and grace, hang it on the hatstand behind my desk, give the little primrose which is part of my inheritance a little water, collect from the shelves what I believe I shall need for the day, and sit down at my desk to do some reading. Every morning.

Every morning in winter after some time the heating will find itself turned on a little more by me, after my fingers have grown cold from clutching a tome of commentary of some sort. A dry and partial warmth emanates with an orange glow of self-content from the electric radiator in the fireplace behind me, making my back insufferably hot, while my hands still remain cold. Every morning in summer after some time the window will go up a little bit to let in a sniff of fresh air.

Every morning at eleven I get up to prepare my morning tea, run two cups of cold water into Russell, as I call him, switch him on, and wait (one minute and a half) until the 'click' tells me that comfort is near. Then, sipping from the gold rimmed cup, I go on with my reading, occasionally allowing myself a biscuit from the tin which I keep on the mantelpiece behind me – one of those tea caddies that have long since fallen into disregard, and which display on their four sides scenes of sailing ships ploughing the waves of a bygone empire, a colourful tea caddie empire of healthy sailors, proud ships, native carriers and ladies sipping cups in their boudoirs.

*

Processions of entries trail before my mental eye and tempt me almost beyond endurance to write down their stories and significances one by one in these accounts, to write a dictionary of my mind. O what wonderful entries they would be: observations on pedestrians, meditations on prayer, inquiries into privacy, plays for Purim, reports from Parliament, treatises on Poles (educated, lower-class, aristocratic, communist, north, south), bulls against popes, rantings on St Paul, notes provoking panic, descriptions of poses, denunciations of piety, analyses of problems, praises for purism, perusals pertaining to pornography, philippics, psalms, proclamations, purrs, programs, profiles, proëmia and postscripts.

I shall resist. My task is too important to be confused with one person and his predilections.

*

Peering out of the window the other day, I had what I can only describe as a revelation. Across the yard, looking to the upper right, I have a partial view of a room on the fourth floor, and there I beheld a vision of the most extraordinary beauty.

She is still there. A woman in a flowery dress is sitting there, a lady of radiant beauty, the fairest amongst women and a lily amongst thorns. If my scanty knowledge of the publishing house as a whole does not deceive me, she must be working somewhere between K and N, probably in M. This makes us kindred spirits. M is the nasal relative of P, which is itself technically a terminus, or unvoiced stop. They are connected through B, the sonar, or voiced stop. The lady in M[13] and my modest self are therefore not really strangers. In correspondence with her floral adornments (she wears the most remarkable dresses with autumn roses), the flowers now appear on the earth and the time of the

---

13 This enigmatic woman has caused considerable disagreement among scholars. Unanimously, Silk and Rover identify her as the lost love of Simmons' earlier days. Mandelbrodt, however, reaches further in his interpretation: 'M is the name of The Mysterious defying the process of analysis within the aesthetic-erotic suddenness of the Thou, the dark Lady of Mystery, the ugly self-consciousness *ex post facto*.'

singing of birds is come, and the voice of a turtle dove is heard in the big tree in the courtyard. (I have never been quite able to understand why these filthy birds are charged with so many associations of peace and love. Their demeanour can only be described as vulgar, with fat and puffed males molesting greyish females in open places. Wherever something beautiful is to be found, these birds appear like a punishment from heaven in vast numbers and defile the whole place with their droppings, occupying every corner with their vile noisiness and the plump flapping of their lumpy wings. With startled and deprecating looks from insolent black button eyes, they seem to pour their mockery on man, who, having created something beautiful for once, is unable to defend it against this invasion of grey barbarism.)

After some experimentation I have found that it is not even necessary to stand by the window in order to behold the Lady. When I sit at my desk and lean out to the far right, across the pile of files, rise from my seat, and press my cheek against the paperwork, I can see her in all her radiance, white and ruddy. (To kiss her – and then to lift up my voice and weep!) Frequently during working hours I now adopt this posture of devotion, in order to return to my work refreshed.

*

Professional interest drives me into antiquarian bookshops

every now and then. You have no idea what treasures can be excavated there for those in my profession. Some books are unexpected gifts of destiny; others, rare and hard to find, are only to be traced by means of patience and cunning. The book which I have been hunting for for years is Reutlin's *Hoechst nutzbar und wertreich Compendium von Wort und Mundart der freyen Bauersleut und auch des Bedelvolks, dargelegt in simpel Manir und versehn auch mit mannigfaltiger Explanation von Gebrauch und Sitte*, which was published in Nurenburg in 1709. It is a compendium of the dialects and demotic expressions of the lower classes in the German-speaking countries during the seventeenth century. Reutlin (1648–1723), the famous grammarian of the south German dialects, and perhaps the father of the scientific investigation of modern languages, made this remarkable work his magnum opus, after having travelled in Germany, Austria, Switzerland and the Netherlands for fourteen years disguised in beggar's clothes. It is an invaluable source of etymology and common usage in the Baroque age. Unfortunately no major library possesses a copy, and the book has been missing since it was stolen from the library of the University of Jerusalem, to which it was bequeathed by the late Prof. Siegfried Rosenstrauch. It is mentioned and commented on in Pierre Menard's excellent monograph *Connections and Affinities between Descartes, Leibnitz and John Wilkins* (Nîmes, 1903), an essay which, as you may be aware, deals largely with aspects of the possibility of the formalization of language. Once I found a copy and was about to buy it from an old lady, who had inherited it from her husband and kept it for sentimental reasons, but in the end she refused to sell it, although she was in sore financial need. When I was finally informed of her death, I quickly made contact with her heir, a civil servant in the Inland Revenue, only to find that he had given all the possessions of his late aunt to a charitable organization, where I lost the trail of the book. It was pure agony. Since then I have been looking for this tome in every bookshop I can find.

I am driven very much indeed to find this book, which would supply me with a wealth of valuable information about words which immigrated into our language by other means than the written word alone. The chase for rare books is a very testing experience, which at times stretches my endurance to the limits and my fantasy at times perhaps rather beyond it. Sometimes the urgency of this search comes over me so strongly that it gives me horrible nightmares. I see myself in an antiquarian bookshop, among high, narrow shelves, holding a treasure of brown, leather-bound books in the twilight of the shop, which does not seem to have walls at all, just shelves, and shelves sloping into indeterminate space. Well-fingered classics, shelves of family Bibles and gold-embossed Waverleys hardly allow me space to move, I push forward in the suffocating, warm, woody, sharp air of old books threatened by rot and worms. In the dim light which seems to come from nowhere I search for assistance, someone to show the way, but the shop-keeper cannot be found. Gradually I realize that the light emanates from a shelf in the far corner, from a book in the middle of a huge pile of tomes lying one upon the other. I move toward it; it is the *Compendium*. It is far up on the top shelf and I can reach it only by heaping books on the floor. I am too short, have to collect more and yet more volumes to stand on, several copies of the Bible, the entire Talmud, various atlases, legal collections, complete works, the scores of Verdi's operas, all under my feet, a mountain of square rockeries, toilsome to climb. I reach up, fail to reach high enough, the floor invisible in the darkness beneath me. I pile more books on the mountain from the top shelves around me, cooking books, old copies of stacks, vile pornographic literature. The dust which comes off every new volume is nauseating, blinding. Gradually my hand moves up to the *Compendium*. Standing on Wagner's *Ring* scores, which I pile upon the trivia of Offenbach and the orations of Wilhelm II, I wriggle towards the book, climb, finger, cautiously. I reach the book and begin to pull it out from underneath the rotting tomes which seem to tower into infinity. I pull and drag, more and more vigorously. Suddenly the book breaks loose and with it the whole pile above it. I am swallowed up by a torrent of paper, flapping, falling, tumbling ever deeper, a cataract of printed words pouring down a dark and horrific canyon, whirling, fluttering pages, snippets, words and fragments. Like frantic birds the falling books infect others with their panic, the torrent of dust and paper rushes on, ever more powerful. The books and bindings hit me hard, I lose the book which I was holding on to, falling, falling into a dark rockery, a chasm of dark bodies.

I awake.

*

Protected by the printed word like an actor by his make-up, I write this account without knowing who is beyond the written page watching me, his likes and dislikes, deviations and normalities, virtues and vices (especially these), tastes and insensitivities. Someone may find it (I will certainly not give it to anybody) and he or she will make its acquaintance in the form of a finger-thick pile of papers covered with erratic scribbles laid down in the pauses between two articles, after lunch, with tea, and on similar occasions. This, this convolution of words and views and sentiments is all you know of me, all you ever may know, will know. A comforting thought. Here at last I can mould myself into a shape which is agreeable. I can make things be true which may be true only for the reader of these pages (a staggering thought: I, concerned with, and almost despairing of finding the objective truth, can generate truth myself quite easily). Whoever looks at my outward appearance, such as the journalist who described me so unmercifully, will not know about this account, the soul-searching of a confused office clerk. People take me for a little boring man; they may take you (worthy reader) for the same, and yet we have a secret world in common, are united in conspiracy.

As in a prayer I cannot be accountable to anyone for what is said here; like a prayer, it is aimed at an audience which may or may not be there, may or may not listen. The mask of printed matter which I wear makes every truth a story, and every story true. However, I deviate from the true subject of these pages, my work; a liberty which must not become a habit. I therefore ask you to excuse my rather inappropriate and unsolicited verbosity.

*

P is the most human letter in the alphabet. It has a character, a life of its own, thousands of years old. It has become a strange friend to me, my councillor and witness, my love and my hatred. All the desirable qualities and the terrible sides of a character are manifest in it. Any good dictionary, an ordinary one, will inform you that the combinations 'ps-' and 'ph-' are merely lodging within the section 'P' out of lexicographic convenience and are really transcriptions of the Greek letters ψ and φ. This is, superficially speaking, true. The deeper reality, however, is that P, the noble outcast among letters, is merely inventive, not to say acquisitive, in the search for peace and happiness among its fellows, a desire to which even the best succumb from time to time. Its ambivalent nature, the dazzling array of words embraced by it, make it stand out from all its peers alone, a suspect element in this community of order and decency. It is too great, too colourful, too contradictory for them, and hence it lives as a pariah in the midst of the neat words around it. P is not too proud to yearn for acceptance, and what it cannot achieve as itself it tries to gain in disguise; by assimilating other letters it hopes also to inherit their healthy normality. Now one could argue about the taste or lack thereof displayed by choosing F and S, but the fact remains that these letters especially are charged with an air of respectability and order. P merely wants to change its name, to move from one neighbourhood to another and start anew. Could it only marry the humble H, B with its domesticity, or even the insignificant little Y, surely it would be one of 'them', and cease to be regarded as the gypsy in the green horse-cart. But as it is, decency is still far off, the matchmaker without success, and so P must inveigle H and S into its realm in order to find some peace. The gods, however, make a mockery of its efforts, and whenever it grabs an H to acquire its decency, the humble one falters under its impact, loses its value and its sound, and leaves even its lover contaminated, turned into a foul F, a farting, foolish Ffff. Nothing is gained, the innocence it had set out to gain defiled and destroyed. Only some of the words that spring from this alliance have got some claim to beauty (many good and beautiful things, like Athena, are born out of monstrosities). Philosophy, for instance, can restore some of its former dignity. Similarly tragic is the case where P tries to adopt with S the majesty of this great letter, rather than humility; it is overridden, disregarded, almost destroyed. Even sadder than with the bastard Ph-, this strange hybrid is open to ridicule and even mockery. P vanishes, cannot prevail against the S, so strong and stern. The Golem which comes hobbling from this mésalliance represents the ultimate failure of regaining respect through masquerade. A hissing sound stings every sensible ear and stabs the pride of P. Psychology! the ultimate make-believe and disregarding of fundamental realities (even of spelling).

Rarely is P ever so well treated, and with such an exquisite mixture of fine tact, insight and erudition, as by the excellent gentleman Mr Psmith (of the Shropshire Smiths), who adopted the letter into his name to be ennobled and elevated above the broad plebs of Smiths. We should all be sincerely grateful to him. But even this gentleman had permanent trouble making his fellow humans understand the silent spelling of his name, and was for its explanation often forced to recite a veritable list of P's most abject failures in the quest for respectability: phthisis, ptarmigan, ptosis, Ptolemaios, Psalm.

We should, from the motivation of intellectual honesty, and in an attempt to honour a great man, forthwith speak of a 'psilent P'.

*

Printed matter becomes literally the basis of my psilent passion. That is to say that I find myself with disturbing frequency leaning across my desk and the files and volumes on it to get a glimpse of the floral apparition which awaits me there. I had no conception that flowery dresses could be so attractive. The comforting red which seems to be the favourite colour of the lady up there has an almost addictive effect on me. All of this happens totally regardless of the fact that the posture which I have to assume is not only very inconvenient, but also most unbecoming for a gentleman of my position and age. Only this morning I was almost inadvertently occupying my observing position when Malakh, after knocking repeatedly, burst into the room. I could hardly make a convincing case of my having had to reach for a remote file and the situation was potentially most embarrassing. I do not intend to behave in a manner which I can myself only describe as immature, nor indeed do I approve of it, but from its secret places of the stairs, in another wing of the building, the flowery dress exercises a power over me which I can only describe as disturbing.

*

Pathetic as my cloister-like life may seem to an outsider, somewhere in the chaos of a metropolis or in the small world of a provincial town, I am a happy man, happy within reason. I have a job which is both satisfying and of considerable importance, an office of my own, nothing to complain of in the least. You may object by telling me that you have long since seen through my literary guise. Indeed I do not wish to insult your intelligence and education by assuming that you have not yet realized that I use these literary devices only for entertaining myself by telling stories. I would never dream of imposing my version of the events in this building on you as the reality; still, everything taken into account, I do maintain that it serves a common interest, since you would in no way be interested in a boring account of a boring person, and therefore it may be much wiser for me in every respect to tell you the truth about something interesting; after all, the last thing you want to hear about, believe me, is my life, which is much like the next man's, and certainly not fit to excite the interest of any publisher, not even worth writing about, let alone filling a book with.

On the other hand I must insist that I do not betray the principles of scholarship and intellectual honesty. As to the first, nobody can accuse me of being insincere by employing myths, since they are exactly what scholarship normally thrives on, even if they are named differently, 'the self-evident', for instance. Myth is at the basis of every life, and to recognize it as such is far from a deviation from intellectual honesty and the pursuit of knowledge.

Here I sit, middle-aged, bourgeois, engaged in an extraordinary and yet normal story, an everyday story, one that happens every day. I please myself with telling these facts of an unreal life, adding to the bare facts only the poor and rudimentary eloquence which I pride myself in all modesty on possessing. This may be the secret of my unilateral relationship with the lady in M. After having watched her in her radiance and returned to my seat and my proper position, regaining my dignity in the stages of tucking in my shirt, pulling down my waistcoat, adjusting my tie, and superficially running a hand through my sparse hair, the image of the wonderful woman up there shines more beautifully than ever. My imagination, coming to assist the glimpse of a dress or a cheek which I have had, creates an ideal, a goddess out of what in all rationality and with my appalling eyesight could just as well be a tailor's mannequin or a red curtain. Without imagination, the eloquence of the mind, all I see is just that: a red bit of dress, or perhaps even a piece of drapery on the window there. Only the holy imagination makes me know the truth that up there is She-of-the-thousand-flowers, a woman whom to claim I would joyfully work for seven years. And there, in my mind, she thrives and takes on a quite independent and wonderful existence. The sense of possibility, a basic principle in my life, exalts her and lifts her up to the realm of eternal beauty, lends her radiance, life and grace, and things become very real which my short-sightedness alone would have prevented me from noticing: her fairness and her dove's eyes (as the saying goes), her slightly stretched little finger when she raises a cup of tea, the very distracting fact that her bust is glowing from beneath the redness of her flowery dress, feeding among its lilies, contributing to her radiance considerably, the little golden ring on her finger (which arouses my apprehension, even jealousy), the soft fluffy hairs on her upper lip which shine so very beautifully in the evening sun, all this is the reality of my imagination, to which I owe so much, and without which the lady in M, the flowering lily among the thorns, might just as well be a wig on a stick.

*

Peas seem to have been decreed by some remote deity to be the backbone of my diet. In the little café where I take my lunch they are always there. The way there is by now well known and very dear to me. Day by day small changes in the windows bear witness to the change going on around me: a new and richly laced display in the lingerie shop makes a half-hearted attempt at maintaining the subtle balance between attractiveness and decency (always to the disadvantage of the former), special blossoms appear next to the perennial roses in the flower shop, the little bookshop on the corner tries to excite the interest of an increasingly illiterate multitude of passers-by with another window full of cloth-bound classics, travel accounts, autobiographies and historical scandals. Only the plumber's display never seems to concede to any idea of change and keeps the same range of vaguely distasteful and polished objects in the public eye as ever.

The establishment itself is Braun's Hof, one of these public places for which no adjective extant ever seems entirely appropriate. When it was founded even the oldest of the staff do not remember, but from its interior it is evident that different proprietors had different ideas as to its vocation, purpose and standing. Little crystal lustres on the wall, one of them still with a dark red (and by now burned) lampshade, as well as solemn prints of landscapes with grazing cows and shepherds and old castles, seem to indicate a bygone time of solid respectability, even elegance. The furniture with all its ghastly practicality indicates a shift in the clientèle, and finally the newly acquired decorations, mainly plastic flowers, witness the present landlord's practical predilections. The name of the place seems not to be local, and may suggest that at some point immigrants were connected with its fate. (I could, however, state nothing with authority, since the name does not even touch my department and I am consequently ignorant of its history.)

Today the café is mainly patronized by the working and lower middle classes, if you will allow me to apply these essentially meaningless labels for the sake of convenience. A great many faces, a stock of urban types and aberrations cast in flesh, find their way to this spot time and again, drawn to it perhaps by the force of sympathy and alikeness. I myself have established myself here mainly as an observer of human life and of what passes for it, and because the location of the halls and its moderate prices are a great convenience for me.

Generations of smokers have combined their efforts in giving the wall a warm hue of honey and the effect is most fortunate. By no means of the offending uniformity of other walls, the shades of yellow to light brown concentrate in corners and on the ceiling, leaving some brighter and rectangular spaces where pictures used to hang which the

77

owner now presumably has sold *ad majorem pecunii gloriam*. Some of the devoted breed of chain smokers still come here to follow their vocation, patiently sitting at some table and in the course of an afternoon dissolving long hours into smoke, filling one aluminium ashtray apiece. The waiter, when he comes by, which is not all that often, will pick up an ashtray and, with a gesture of nonchalant boredom, empty it onto his tray only to crash it back onto the table.

The waiter. He is a man in his eternal sixties (perhaps the timeless son of our never-ageing porter) miserable with displeasure at the constant presence of intruding and disturbing guests. He does not make a secret of the fact that he would prefer to have the place to himself, and to finish his cigarette, which is always glowing away on the counter, and which he sucks greedily every free moment. Always busy, he is constantly causing upheaval in some corner of the room by squeezing himself through between two particularly close chairs, snorting 'cuseme!' as if it were an insult. No moment seems to go by without the waiter carrying something from one place to another – ashtrays, newspapers, plates, menus, change, cigarettes, enormous trays laden with cups of coffee. Still this modern Sisyphus not only fails to bring any order into the scattered remains on the small plastic-topped tables (I have long since suspected him of keeping a certain number of items constantly on his tray without ever taking them off), but also takes a considerable time acknowledging a guest's attempt to lodge his order, three times longer before he is finally rewarded for his patience. In the moment least suspected by the meanwhile dozing guest the order will finally be deposited upon the table with considerable force, leaving the recipient too bewildered to ask for any supplement or alteration before the spectre has disappeared again. The only way of getting my meal in good time is, as I found out, to establish contact with the kitchen-maid, who occasionally goes round to collect some plates for washing up, something the waiter does not find time for at all. When she glides by, very much sixteen, cheeks rosy with youth, it is prudent to ask her for the meal on today's menu. It will appear some ten minutes later. The food is always solid, never really good, never changing in composition: chips & pies & peas.

*

Providence was kind when it placed P between O and Q. As if to mock the noble letter's aspirations to wholeness and respectability, it was stuck between two letters which in their very form symbolize wholeness. Still, even if O may appear to be the egg-shaped principle of beginning itself, it is P which is the real and only first letter of the alphabet. In Hebrew, a language traditionally seen as importing deeper truths, the letter 'Pé' denotes also 'mouth', and indeed the first utterances from the mouth of any infant will be 'Papa' and 'Mama' which of course are morphologically closely related.[14] P is the very beginning of all human speech, a fact which may contribute to the envy of the other letters.

*

Po-faced plutocrats seem to be the rulers of this world in every dominion and so it is not surprising that even the Dictionary is cursed with a board of governors. People who are profoundly ignorant of the beauty and importance of our work rule the workings of the publishing house with the decorum of stock-in-trade officialdom and brainless correctness. These half-witted accountants of salvation work doggedly on their own lines, oblivious of the existence of staff or even Dr Javis, and pour out regulations, supplications, recommendations, decrees, prohibitions, reprimands without pause. They are a class of potent parvenus, grey, semi-detached people, who unwittingly perform a grotesque pantomime of power. The rules made by the board of governors do not follow any necessity but the overriding regulation that there must be at least sixteen new decrees a day. Most of these occur and vanish far too quickly to make their observance possible, but from time to time a new and senseless regulation hits the offices. The board of governors is elected by the board of governors alone, and only death can terminate membership. Anyone

---

14 For a detailed documentation of this see: R. Taubstumm and K. Niemowa, *Infant Speech and Brain Development*, Cambridge, Mass., 1987, pp. 386–97.

who is a retired banker and claims to be the most-music-loving-person-in-the-world is eligible. The latter prerogative, introduced to maintain a certain stability, leads to lengthy feuds and the exchange of cold civilities among the governors; scores are decided by the number of opera tickets bought, the number of hours endured in an opera. I see them every day at half past five, flooding out of the building in grey suits, little bold men, hurrying home to do some gardening and social spanner-in-the-works (a game which is, as far as I am informed, not unlike bowling), their favourite pastime.

*

Possibly you find me repetitive, but I feel I must refer again to the subject of new word coinages, especially since nowadays the world is swamped day by day with new bastardizations. Let me therefore call just one witness, who will make the case for me: Immanuel Kant, that great philosopher and master of language and style. He wrote (in the *Critique of Pure Reason*, Transcendental Logic, Dialectic II, 1st book, 1st part, p. 245):

> To coin new words is a pretension towards legislation in languages which rarely succeeds, and before one goes to this desperate measure, it is prudent to look around in a dead and erudite language, whether not thither the concept together with its fit expression is to be found; and if the old usage has become somewhat uncertain through carelessness of its authors, it is

nevertheless better, to make the firm meaning, which pertained to it (even if it is doubtful that people had even that in their mind), than to spoil one's enterprise by rendering oneself obscure.

I rest my case. Kant, with his characteristic lucidity and mastery of style, has put authoritatively exactly what I wanted to express in my own inadequate words.

*

Poetry and Prose are the objects of my existence as an editor. Selected P[oetry] and P[rose], complete P & P, collected P & P, antique P & P, sublime P & P, sentimental P & P. P & P is my B & B, my bread and butter, my bed and breakfast, always available for immediate survival, always only for the short term. Foreign lodgings seldom tailored to my comfort, strange homes to be inhabited by paying guests, seldom too dear to leave, often too dear to pay. They are the conditions in which I survive. To write! What an ambition to have, to pen one's ambitions all on the great patriarchs and prostitutes of literary strife, P & P; pondering, penetrating, preserving – perishing. Then I return to the safe haven of the Communications, on which I am quite an expert now. If I cannot do any truly constructive work I might as well work out what others think about it. I proceed to search for the method, always arrive at the penultimate step, forever the penultimate.

P can be imposing and preposterous. Sometimes I feel practically pounced upon by its sheer force and demand for
attention. Pages of words and chains of letters drag around
on the desk before me, P-words, each with its history, etymology and significance. At times my scholarship almost
surrenders to the impact of the countless words and characters, and I feel my mind waver and my firmness tremble.
This brings me to perhaps the most regrettable incident in
my career as an editor – the memorable evening when I,
carried away by an ecstasy which had suddenly overcome
me, mistook good old Malakh for a complete stranger and
started to engage in a wrestling bout with him, yelling nonsensical demands. The poor man was quite helpless and
tried to calm me down, with mixed success, as I will relate
later. Needless to say I was utterly embarrassed when I
regained my normal consciousness, and I can hardly praise
Malakh enough for taking the incident so well (he did not
even mention it). A marvellous fellow (though I do remember that he at one point in this sorry event called me various
names, but this may also have been an hallucination). The
incident which prompted my lapse (the only one), and I
hesitate to bring it to my memory again for fear it might be
still too strong, was some historical research into the word
'pleasure'.

I have already had the opportunity of relating a similar
incident, albeit on a smaller scale. This occurrence, however,

was of an entirely different proportion. In order to make you understand the true nature of the incident, I will have to deviate from my usual strict procedure of telling facts and facts only, and adopt some of the methods of the story-telling profession. As I am a scientist I am naturally hesitant to use my pen in the way of novel-writers and the like, but in this case I feel compelled to do so, as without recreating the incident I fear I cannot explain what really happened. I do not harbour the illusion of being able to evoke the full anguish suffered by me in the midst of this Babel mumbling, babbling and shrieking of voices from the past; I do not even want to bring the shattering voices back too true to life for fear I might not be able to stand it. At the time when they occurred, I was quite sure that the voices were truly present in my room, speaking from the corners, lurking behind the desk, singing from the courtyard, echoing in the black depth of the fireplace, which turned into a veritable furnace of cacophony. The ensuing polylogue (for lack of a better word) seemed to be a terrible fight between an old jester of the basest humour and voices which seemed to come from the recesses of the fireplace, and which quickly filled the whole room with gibberish. Sitting at my desk, reading the history of the word in question, I heard from the door:

– please, sir!

and rising to see who I would find there, I heard from behind me, from the hatstand, seemingly from under my own hat, aping my voice,

– good e'en your worship!

I sat transfixed. The conversation of unseen voices pro-
ceeded with ever increasing speed, from all corners and
edges of the room.

- At your pleasure!
- So pleased to meet you.
- Please the pigs!!
- What pigs please?
- *Alexander the pig!*
- The great!
- Great pleasure.
- *I peseech you heartily!*
- Pardon?
- Please what?
- *It's out of my prains!*
- Wilt please tou go?
- By pleasure or pain I would be understood to
  signify . . .
- *O you?! PUGGER OFF!!*
- Prave words.
- PLEASE!
- Whom do I have the pleasure of talking to?
- Butoones of ladies of pleasure.
- Please yourself
- Please it, your holiness, I think it be some ghost!
- *Ay, he was porn in Mornmouth.*
- Please the Lord,

- *I peg your . . .*
- It is the so-called pleasure-pain-principle.
- Now judge if herein be pleasure.
- Plese it, Lorde, to that thou defendeth me.
- Ye shall have all you plese!
- Please refrain!
- For God wasteth the bones of those that plesen to man.
- To pleasure, his daily whim!
- *Pehold the Lord*
- O pleasure, you're indeed a pleasant thing.
- Which pleasure please?
- Parson's pleasure.   – Punting!
- God's plood and his . . .   – Si vobis placet.
- Please   – The pepil was plesed with his faire speeche.
- Pleasure?
- Perhappes they will please themselves upon her . . .
- Pless . . .
- Please the pigs with pearls!   – Please, pleasure, I hold on to your hellish heels
- It's my pleasing, prave words, please the pigs, PLESS, my pleasingplease not, Plymouth north Biscay, west or north-west, four or five, moderate or good[15] old

---

15 Here Mandelbrodt finds his view confirmed that the text disintegrates its own components: 'As pieces of ships destroyed, the words are borne to Plymouth and Biscay on the waves of self-consciously re-orienting equivocalities.'

man, nay, be not angry, I am pleased, plessed, my
plessing, heavenly stranger, at my plesir, pleasing
my plessing, stranger.
PLESS!

At this point I came to with a sharp pain in my leg, since
in his efforts to calm me, Malakh had pushed me firmly to
the ground, and my hip was trapped under the desk and
sprained (a fact, incidentally, which still compels me to
carry a walking stick). Malakh stood over me and appealed
to me urgently:

– Please, wake up, heavens, please, please!

*

Probably the most misunderstood and underestimated of
the sciences, lexicography still suffers from so many
internal controversies and disagreements about its basic
principles and procedure that it is exceedingly difficult to
make any progress whatsoever, which is acknowledged by
other scholars in the field.

For centuries the finest minds in ancient Greece, Europe,
the Arab countries and India have pondered questions of
lexicography and grammar without reaching a final consen-
sus. From Apollinus Apocryphus (453–302 BC) to modern

minds such as Chomsky[16] and Klumsky,[17] various models and methods have been drawn up, tried, and discarded, most of them on technical grounds which I cannot recount without succumbing to the danger of engaging in a discourse incomprehensible to the layman (a temptation few specialists are able to resist). All these attempts, however, have been made without any knowledge of MS 62.7 Sem 3.[18] This invaluable document is an early Semitic manuscript, fragments of which are now lodged in the library of the British Museum in London (sections 3–5; the name of the manuscript today is the library signature of this largest surviving fragment), in the Jagellonian University at Cracow (section 6), the Bodleian Library, Oxford University (sections 7–9), and the University of Jerusalem (section 10). The long and troubled history of this document in modern times is inextricably connected with the name Jan Potocki (1761–1815). Potocki, a Pole who was brought up in the Ukraine and in Switzerland, one of the most brilliant minds of the eighteenth and early nineteenth centuries, had a keen interest in languages, of which he spoke eight fluently. After early studies in Vienna he began his career as an officer and served in Africa and the Mediterranean, where he was

---

16 Noam Chomsky, (1928–   ), American linguist.
17 Henry D. Klumsky (1936–1962), American linguist, his contribution to linguistics is still underestimated, perhaps partly because of his tragic and untimely death.
18 A scientific edition of this document is now being prepared by scholars at Yale University, to be published in Spring 2029.

deployed hunting pirates off Malta. Already at this time he had begun to research African influences on the Italian language, and later on the culture of Turkey, where he lived for some years and where he found his valet Osman, from whom he was to become inseparable. His interest in the Levant, which he had travelled extensively, and in its culture, never ceased, and he often appeared dressed *a la turca*. Later in his career, and after his return to Europe, he became fascinated with the idea of Slavdom and set out to write a comprehensive and comparative grammar of the Slavonic languages with special consideration of the Lusatian Sorbs, a Slavonic tribe living in Germany. After some time as a prominent figure in the political and cultural life of Poland, he moved to France, but was soon disillusioned with the ambitions and methods of his Jacobean friends. He travelled in Spain and Morocco, before finally moving to Russia, where he served as personal advisor to the Russian Minister of Foreign Affairs, with whom he was personally acquainted. From St Petersburg Potocki set out on an expedition to China, but was refused entry into the country. On returning from this journey Potocki wrote his only novel, *A Manuscript found in Saragossa*, a work still cherished by connoisseurs. Always tending to fits of depression, Potocki had made a habit of filing down the knob of his silver samovar during such times. When eventually the knob had reached the desired size, he loaded the silver bullet into his dueling pistol and shot himself. The scientific heritage which Potocki left was a rich one and has not yet been fully exploited: the *Research on Sarmatia* (Warsaw, 1789–92) and the *Historical and Geographic Fragments of Scythia, Sarmatia and the Slavs* (Germany, 1796) have received no scholarly attention at all, the *Prehistory of the Peoples of Russia* (St Petersburg, 1802) very little. It was on one of his travels in the Levant that Potocki bought an old manuscript from an Arab peddler who claimed to have found it in the ruins of a house in Safed, in northern Palestine. Potocki brought the find with him to Amsterdam, and left the largest part of it with a friend, the eminent Henk van der Uffelen, a specialist in Semitic dialects, for closer inspection (the remainder, which Potocki took to Poland, is today in Cracow). Weeks later, van der Uffelen was robbed, and fragments of the stolen manuscript appeared subsequently in England and Germany. Unable to reclaim the lost treasure, the Dutch scholar felt unable to face Potocki ever again, and became a sailor in the Dutch merchant navy. The fate of the manuscript, however, had not yet reached its nadir. Being mistaken for two distinct texts, the English fragment was ripped apart and sold to two different libraries, the British Library and the Bodleian Library at Oxford University. At the British Library the manuscript (sections 1–5) lay disregarded for some twenty years, and was then used by a bookbinder as material for the bindings and restoration of other volumes. When the terrible error was discovered in 1953, several attempts were made by outstanding scholars and restorers to save what could be saved, but it was too late to rediscover all the fragments used. Fragment 3 was

found in the lining of an eleventh-century English manuscript, the 'Alesbury Psalter'; fragment 4 resurfaced in the
binding of the 'Parliamentary Journal, Winter 1887–88'
together with a previously unknown fragment from an
illuminated Hebrew manuscript from the ninth century;
and fragment 5 was found unused in a disused storage
room. The first two fragments must be regarded as lost
forever.

The Oxford fragment, MS 62.7 Sem 3 Ox, is known only in
the translated version by W. R. Whitney, which appeared
in the 1853 issue of the *Proceedings of the Royal Oriental
Society* (No. 3, pp. 271–302) under the title *A Hymn to the
Sun from Ancient Palestine: Evidence for Linguistic Change*. The
author, a known eccentric, claims to have found in this text
proof of the fact that the Scottish people descended from the
tribe of Reuven, but this hypothesis is not undisputed
among his colleagues. The original of the fragment was
unfortunately lost in Oxford's stacks and is not retraceable,
since the catalogue of the Bodleian Library lists only
author's names, and the manuscript in question is anony-
mous. Consequently, no one has ever seen it since Whitney
translated it in 1853.

As far as the content of the text can be reconstructed, it is
a hymnical dialogue between the prophet Daniel and an
angel (believed by other scholars to be a martyred saint) on
the nature of creation and the prayers said by the angels.
This part especially is in fact a concealed treatise on the
nature of language (n.b. the Jerusalem fragment, MS 62.7

Sem 3 Jer) and the possibility of codifying words. As far as is known, the Cracow fragment (MS 62.7 Sem 3 Cra) which, because of the prevailing political situation, is not very well documented in the west, introduces a new element, the temptation of Daniel by a demon, Sa'-sûer, who claims that language is not at all made by God and is in fact quite arbitrary and subject to change (the fact that this fragment is unlike the other known parts suggests that we are here dealing with a later redactorial addition). Finally, Daniel emerges as the hero and overcomes the demon; the manuscript closes with the hymn translated by Whitney in 1853. (This at least is the order which Prof. Edelstein of Chicago has established and documented well with parallel texts from the same tradition.)

This then is the document which has been the constant source of inspiration and discussion in the Great Academy. Needless to say, the various uncertainties in the interpretation of words and concepts, ambiguities in the history of particular notions and other problems of this kind contribute greatly to the liveliness of the disputes. The yield, however, is enormous: the possibilities of seeing language as, well, as something which is what it is, and the ensuing concepts and options open out a whole new world of methods and observances. The wealth of ideas and knowledge contained in the Communications is the reason that studying them is of crucial importance to my profession; I know that I will find the method which is concealed in it.

*

Peni-el is the place in the Bible where Jacob struggled with the angel and was renamed. Is Peni-el a word demanding recognition? If so, why the unnerving inconsistency of calling the place Penu-el just one verse later? According to the Communications, where this problem was discussed as well, the two versions are only two sides of one coin, for, as they maintain, Jacob cannot speak for himself alone after his fight, but has to speak for his whole people. This I find very difficult to understand. The problem remains: which version shall we adopt?

*

            PAAAA –   Pom![19]
      po po pa   po
    pom   po
Pom pom,   plommm

Have you already realized that P has a very special ring to it? Every little tune proves it. How different this one would be, if someone were to sing it to 'ratatataa' or 'la la la' or anything else. P is an intimate letter, musical. Yes, it is

19 The tune notated here has been described by various scholars as the *Internationale*, the American national anthem, *Heil Dir im Siegerkranz*, a Sufi-hymn, and as the second theme in Beethoven's Fifth Symphony.

explosive, but it is also very close and friendly; Milne's famous bear could not have been given any name starting with a different letter. It is the letter of children, wise men – and stutterers. The latter often fight a hard and terrible fight with it, their faces twisting into all sorts of cruel contortions, changing in colour from red to blue and then pale, their audience desperately trying to avert their gaze in embarrassment, a horrendous, ppp-p,-pff-p-p-p-painful experience. It can be a terrible tyrant, as can any great personality. Pompous and pampering, private and proud. Pooh – and Piglet.

*

Permitting myself perhaps rather more than what is appropriate (for fear of not being allowed, I have not looked up what the Communications have to say about this matter), I have finally taken action. This morning, before even starting my work, I have with all my strength jerked the right-hand corner of the desk about ten inches forward; the result is spectacular. I can now see the Lady in M without even moving from my place. With a tiny lowering of my head I have what can only be described as a perfect view into the room upstairs. A playful spring sun has now begun to paint all sorts of patterns onto the flowery dress in there. In the morning I can distinctly see the lady's neck in the lower window partition, and when she moves to reach for a new file – a precious moment – her head. When this happens, her hair shines in the warm chestnut colour of a Flemish painting; the light, gliding down her ivory neck, gives radiance to her delicate skin, which flows smoothly until it borders the roses and lilies of the flowering dress. O these flowers of spring! An orchard of pomegranates!

In the winter this flowering dress was a centre of beauty and consolation for me. When nothing blossomed and nothing thrived, a single glimpse up to her window, to the ever-flowering beauty over there, an enclosed garden, regardless of the season, promised another spring.

The same spring sun which lends the lady extra radiance entertains itself by creating all sorts of effects on the wall opposite my desk. Around noon a bright rectangle will appear by the floor, and gradually travel upwards, drawing ever more golden landscapes of shadows and mysterious shapes. The shadows of the branches of the big tree in the courtyard provide the repertoire of forms and silhouettes which for moments seem to transform the upright wall into a threatening barrier of cliffs. Finally, in the evening, it summons up a red inferno of flames licking on the ceiling, which seem to elevate the solid masonry beyond my reach and leave me under this overbearing canopy of terrible beauty until it slowly dies into the comforting light of the reading lamp on my desk.

Then the whole world is contracted into one single plane ablaze with light, an open tome of the Communications mostly, black letters coming to life in solemn processions of petrified gestures, trailing across the plain of gleaming white. There is nothing, nothing exists outside this light, nothing apart from the sea of strangely lively characters, and of two hands tracing the meandering movements of the discussions and heated arguments, wonderfully alone with their opinions and contradictions, left to the enjoyment of utter beauty. The world tranquilly concentrated into the majesty of reason, into black flames of reasoning, dancing courtly dances on the floor of white marble which lies prepared for them. My hands follow the figures and ritual bows, the steps and pirouettes of the symbols, knowing that somewhere in their pavanes, allemandes, polonaises and courantes lies the secret that informs their movements.

*

Phantasms and dreams are constantly in the way of solid, single-minded editorial work. Not so long ago, when looking up some references for the word 'place', I fell asleep and had a very curious dream indeed. I had just got as far as the sentence 'And he lighted upon a certain place, and tarried there all night,' in a classical but little-read text, when I dozed off. My dream took me to the porter's lodge, and I found myself sitting in there, lit by the single dim lightbulb and surrounded by assorted *bric a brac*. The staircase in the hall in front of me was swollen to enormous proportions, reaching right up to the high office, and on it hundreds and hundreds of clerks and office messengers ran busily up and down like so many excited ants. Assuming that there must have been an emergency, I searched my compartment for the alarm, but could not find it. I dialled the number of the high office on the internal phone, but nobody had heard of an emergency, and I was told instead not to neglect the work which had been given to me. Looking around in the lodge, I found that it was filled with dusty files, all belonging to my department. When I examined them closely, I found that they were all dealing with names of places: Paddington, Port Said, Pangaea, Pembroke, Parramatta, Peenemünde, Persia, Petersburg, Philippi, Palestine, Pishpek, Paris, Poland, Porcupine, Pabianice, Prussia, Paisley, Pushkin and Putumayo. I awoke to find that I had indeed slept with my head on files with geographical names. Still, I do wish the work would not affect me so strongly.

*

Prairies. Any enterprise such as the Dictionary must necessarily be dubious and obscure in the eyes of the great crowd of scholars ignorant of its true aims, its methods and its goals. They prefer to follow the well trodden paths of established scholarship, of schools of thought with their enemies and epigones, without ever running the risk of making a true discovery. Caravans of learning engaged in excited gibberish follow the old way into no man's land, to an oasis long since exhausted and far removed from the society they set out to find and describe, while in between their thin paths is the vast *terra incognita* of human knowledge, which nobody dares to enter. Some are courageous, brave steps into the vast desert. Most fall prey to starvation; others, having felt the merciless bite of the sun, hurry back to the track they left. Only a few carry on, doggedly, regardless of scorn at the outset, and of hardship during their travels. Solitary, they wander off, away from the caravans which are engulfed in their own babbling contradictions, substantiations, argumentations, citations, refutations, their circling investigations. The lonely traveller looks for an oasis, guided only by intuition, knowing that it is his fate to be either a disregarded discoverer or an outright charlatan. The caravan which he left now nothing but a cloud on the horizon, he walks on, knowing neither what to search for nor where. In abandoning the rules of orthodox scholarship, I myself am such an explorer. In my search for a map of the territory which nobody has ever entered, I cling to the Communications; there I may find the way.

*

Perhaps you remember my telling you about the small café in which I usually take my lunch. Something almost happened there.

To appreciate the incident properly, you have to evoke the scene and atmosphere: in a place like this, where the stingy life of small people grinds the furniture for years and years on end, everything seems to be faded, yellowed. It is as if the cigarette smoke which continually rises to the ceiling, like incense in a burnt offering to some strange tribal deity, has not only tinted the ceiling and the walls with nondescript hues of yellow and brown, but permeated everything with the taste of faded and cheap pleasures. The chequered floor does not offer quite contrasting colours, and looks as if it had been trodden out even before being trodden on; assorted broken chairs miraculously still support their occupants. The plastic surfaces of the little tables are scrubbed and scratched with a thousand lines like veteran desks in an old school. The pots of plastic flowers which are dangling from the pillars have long since lost their synthetic liveliness and taken on the lighter tone of cooked vegetables. Their grime does not vanish with polishing (which happens every evening or so) or washing (every Monday morning).

According to the notice by the door, the cakes and sandwiches are freshly made every day, and yet they never look fresh; even the loud apron of the fleshy matron seems to merge into the general dull despondency. The greyish brown of the tea, here called white without any conscious irony, poured from a gigantic aluminium pot into whitish cups, seems to bear the colour to which the whole place aspires. Even the patrons of the establishment take on these characteristics. The kitchen maid (an inmate rather than a patroness), pretty, almost unbearably youthful, is somehow camouflaged into the place, even if the premature and theatrical make-up on her vaguely Slavonic face would be striking in another place, even if her stout little legs in net stockings speak out with unmistakable femininity from between the nothing of a black skirt and the knee-high leather boots. Even the traffic wardens, who always occupy the far right-hand corner of the room, apparently never doing anything else, seem not as aggressively black-and-white as they look outside. Everything is subdued. The traffic wardens have their HQ in this establishment. They are the incarnation of righteousness, broadly filling the bench and chairs around one table; their paraphernalia of lawfulness scattered around them, they seem to be the rightful owners of everything around. They are not the only regulars here (one comes to know them). There is the little elderly man who always sits alone at one small table, toothless and perpetually chewing, his face collapsing, each time he closes his jaws, into almost nothing but a pair of eyes and a curiously dislodged nose, staring in front of him and mourning some long-forgotten loss. There are the buddies (I do not have any more respectful and yet equally fitting designation for them), three men who come when I am about to leave and sit down, each with a glass of beer. A smallish man with an outlived pinstriped jacket; another small man, fat, with a thin coat of black hair glued to the skull, his red face in stark contrast (as far as this place allows it) with his greyish tie; a tall man with equally dark hair which always sports a streak of white at the parting. They converse in the way of people who have known one another for decades, uttering catch-phrases, mumbling well-known commentaries on well known things and unchanging problems, faintly enjoying each other's company, which seems to recall the days when the collected soliloquies amounted to conversations, and the greedy glances at the kitchen maid produced excitement, perhaps even adventure.

Housewives at another table keep alive the illusion of really talking to one another. They thrash out every bit of news, comfortably settled on chairs which seem too diminutive under enormous behinds really to be able to bear them. Great big bare forearms gesticulate and small hands hold tiny cups; cakes stand ready to contribute to the sweet immensity. Sometimes a meagre little lady is among them, a sister, treated with pity and respect, who sips her tea with a slightly extended little finger, and listens to the snippets of gossip and jellied opinion shooting and rolling to and fro. – You ought to be ashamed, I says, really. – I didn't mince my words, I said to her myself . . . – And no more can't I, I said. – My word! – I said: you are a proper fool.

The clatter of chatter from a colourless within, pierced by the screaming of the coffee machine, and outside, behind the big windows like an aquarium, the silent world, with the greengrocer's lads and the green green greens and the luminous apples and oranges.

On my way to the café I pass a butcher's shop, and every day he has a pig's head in his window. They look peaceful and resigned, these pigs, eyes shut, sometimes badly bruised, flapping pink ears (20p apiece) with white hair around them like a halo, and in between, stuck into the thick skin of the skull, a little notice, '£1 each'.

Something almost happened.

Sitting there, between the old man and the whitebread housewives and the traffic wardens, all monochrome people, faded characters, I saw the door open, and then, at the counter, turning her back towards me, a flowery dress, radiant in its splendour like the vision of a desert saint, glowing colour infusing the whole room with warmth of red, and blue, and green.

Instinctively I leaned wide over the table to the right, across the tea and the residues of a meagre meal (peas), but I could not get a glimpse of her face (instead my head engaged in close encounter with the expanses of one of the housewives), of this face, her face, the face which followed me everywhere. For a little, heavenly while, I closed my eyes to relish this supreme moment, the encounter, then –

She was gone.

– That's the new 'un from the butcher's, said one of the housewives, and their heads around the table were lowered in a silent conference of conspiracy.

*

PASSION – prude petty pusillanimity
PURITY – presumptuous perverse pornocracy
PEACE – plotting patriotic pogroms
POETRY – polemic parody

PRIDE – punishment, penitence

PRAYER – pompous pretentious palaver

Great words, the rulers of their realm, are checked by others, held in uncertainty, suspended by the anarchy of sinister consorts and comrades on adjacent pages. No principle goes without persuasion, no promise without an added 'provided that . . .', a 'perhaps however'. Even on the impartial pages of a dictionary words are, before they are even used, riddled with contradictions, fighting for their survival, desperate to retain their sense and meaning. Paradox seems to be the ruling word, unchallenged by any other, not even by purity, which is itself deeply engaged in a potentially fatal struggle. Nothing that rings out rings true. Mad mixtures and contortions of meaning populate the pages, columns and entries of an encyclopaedia; the words refute themselves.

*

Pictures always induce me to let my imagination wander; even the worst of them (and some of them especially) evoke more than they represent. Opposite my desk, above the bookshelves filled with unread journals (I am an unhappy subscriber to the *Journal of European Linguistics*,[20] the *Advances of the American Semiographic Convention*, the *Revue*

---

20 This journal is not in evidence in the catalogue of the Library of Congress.

Internationale de Jargons Académiques, the *Tijdschrift voor het Nederlandsche Bijwoord*, the excellent Hebrew series *ha-Pilpul*, the *Cambridge Review of Unnecessary Adjectives*, and the *Zeitschrift der Heidelberger Adorno-Gesellschaft für Sprachmißbrauch*) opposite my desk, there is a picture which is especially dear to me. I found it in one of those little antique shops in our capital between maps of old cities and etchings of little known African tribes, ripped out of old dictionaries. Amidst these assorted horrors I was surprised to find an original engraving of Davide Le Compte,[21] the little known French artist, who, before anyone else, devoted himself exclusively to his fascination for abstract forms and symbols. It is a representation of two letters, which, true to Renaissance fashion, are constructed on geometrical lines, rather like the famous da Vinci drawing of a man enclosed in a circle and a square. The characters thus constructed are P and S.[22] I have no idea why the artist chose these two letters rather than others, but the harmonious lines and circles which define them had such a soothing effect on me

---

21 Davide Le Compte (1597–1643), French engraver.
22 Mandelbrodt writes about the picture in question: 'PS is Simmons' existential chiffre, denoting the Post-scriptum on modernity. It is the very insignia of after-culture and the profound impossibility of writing in the face of humankind's invincible enslavement to the oppressive superhuman persona of the absent God.' A. Rover, on the other hand, writes: 'The unidentified main character of the manuscript points us here, tongue in cheek, back to his author, by using his initials: P[aul] S[immons].'

that I immediately bought it, and now always keep it in my office.

In a frame of heavy gold, which with its curves and ornaments lends the most interesting contrast to the strictness of the construction, the picture is a constant pleasure to my eyes whenever they wander from the small print of the Communications. I must confess that I have always thought of P as a bit ill-balanced (one of the few mistakes which betray its unstable character), and this picture makes the point. P, standing on one single pillar, and upholding by some miraculous force an arch, like the remnants of a Hellenistic temple or a tree struck by a thunderbolt, is in its awesome dynamic force tempered by S, the perfect balance, curving like Aesculap's serpent on the other side, engulfed in swaying circles, angle-points and lines. At dusk, when the light becomes less decisive, and allows the mind to fill the fading splendour of the day with its creatures, the lines of the picture start contorting themselves and flowing together, forming new beings, beasts, features and faces. With the silent skill of genius unaware, the two letters perform a nocturnal comedy of twitching eyes, long noses and speaking mouths in a perfect elliptical shape. Some faces in this geometric masquerade appear new with every furtive glance cast at the pictures, others are by now old acquaintances, characters, relations who are near but incomprehensible. Is it just my tired eye which sees these beings on a mute piece of paper, or will the characters, when unobserved, break out of their pencilled chains, evolve from the lines of cosmic order, and finally appear as an uproar of faces in a grotesque world of twenty-four by thirty inches? With every day the faces become more real, speak more distinctly than the letters, which superficially seem to occupy the space.

*

Primary existence, unhinged from the dependency of scholarly pursuits, seems at times to be the central aim in life. My existence as editor is by its very definition invisible, secondary, slowly dissolving into footnotes and critical appendices, absorbed into commentaries and learned disputations. On a day in a future perhaps not too distant, perhaps emphatically lauded by other scholars, themselves already half-vanished into the literature written about them, and by them about somebody, something else, my tombstone will bear the name of a hundred entries and commentaries, not mine. A scholar lives a mediated life, feeding on the arguments of others, the knowledge and errors of his kin. He has no feet to stand on, but walks about on stilts of acquired knowledge, surveying from his lofty heights the world above which he is so strangely elevated.

Many a scholar, unable to root himself within the breathing and heaving, brooding matter of the immediate world from which he has been abstracted, slowly expires in appendices and catalogued files, some of which are veritable graveyards of the learned. Having been taught that individuality is the vice supreme, scholars have drained out their intelligence and diffused what little individuality remained into distinctions, substantiations, qualifications, refutations, and verifications. Handling only the thoughts of others, with no imagination of their own, they dry out progressively, become less and less substantial. The idea that ink flows in scholars' veins can by no means claim originality, but it illustrates the point in question; while romantic poets may sign contracts with the devil with their own blood, scholars and scientists write with ink in their veins, using it up slowly, fading away. The scholar's features become gradually less determinable, he withers, yellows, like the little café from tobacco, in the fumes of his learning, finally he turns quite white, and black spots start to appear all over him. On a certain day it then becomes clear that he who does not possess a character, is in fact made of them. Lines of innumerable characters and letters wind around his extremities like dried vine leaves around a Bacchus made of stone: sub-commentaries on his absent personality, spurious verifications of his existence, bibliographies on neglected possibilities, statistics about his day-by-day routine, obscure monographs on his aberrations, introductions to his merits and achievements. Like a scarecrow fending off every affliction of emotion and every suspected element of personality, he seems to move in the soft breeze of ongoing debate, then slowly the lines disintegrate like grotesquely marked caterpillars, crawl away and take on their own existence in mighty tomes, forgotten volumes,

Festschriften, journals, and dissertations. This illness is well known but not at all documented, since everybody single-minded enough to research it has invariably fallen prey to it.[23] Scholars do not speak openly about this dark threat of leprosy. Fear makes them silent.

There are strategies for avoiding this horrific plague, but only one method has been known to be infallible: no scholar who has produced or done anything which is original and unprecedented, which leaves the harbour of study for the open sea, has ever been afflicted. This fact has caused great anguish to Professors, Doctors and *Privatgelehrter*. They try to write poems, even plays; some wrack their brains for one line, one expression novel in literature, learn musical instruments and give free instruction to the young. Others take on hobbies and silly pastimes in the hope of being thought eccentric: bee-keeping, stamp collecting, amateur drama, snake charming, alcoholism, early music, gardening, Catholicism, conjuring, political careers, nothing which has not yet been tried. A linguist in Copenhagen, who showed the first signs of this terrible illness (footnotes on the toes), was eventually convicted for pederasty after paying a little boy six Krona to suck his toes, in the vain hope that the freshness of the child might expunge the symptoms. He became librarian of the prison in Helsingør,

---

23 The disease has been finally described by two young scientists at
   Strasbourg University, in May 1991, appropriately named 'Simmons'
   Syndrome'. One of the scientists involved has since disappeared.

where he disappeared without trace, to the great embarrassment of the authorities, in the section for popular fiction.
In Leyden, Holland, a professor of numismatics began to
determine scientific questions by tossing coins from the
fourth century BC. He remained completely healthy, but not
without suffering a marked rise in mistrust among his colleagues. The disappearance of the well known Egyptologist
Hans Peter von der Wühl in Marburg attracted the attention
of the press all around the world (even in Austria the papers
covered it) and gave rise to intense speculation about his
alleged involvement with a ring of art thieves. Unknown to
the journalist, and seemingly unconnected with the case, the
library of Marburg University added to its catalogue a work
which had been found in the stacks, and which presented
the librarian with some difficulty, since it had no title and
consisted of footnotes only. A case of happy escape from the
affliction is that of an inorganic chemist in Princeton who
began to translate Joyce into ancient Greek and to write his
articles in flawless hexameters which were much praised by
his colleagues in the Classics department; his professional
standing as a chemist (which had been considerable), however, became somewhat obscured.

*

Painting my age with the beauty of her days, I have begun
to take imaginary tea with the lady in M. Every day at four-
thirty, she has her tea. Before my mental eye I clearly see her

sipping from a fine cup with a gently extended little finger, so every day at this very time I put the kettle on. After one-and-a-half minutes the lid quietly starts dancing (click!), and I can pour my own cup. Then I sit there, slightly leaning to the right in order to obtain a better view, and have tea in a quiet dreamy fashion with the lady of my heart. Every day, unbeknownst to her, she has tea with me – a perfect couple, united in a common cause. Only natural forces can prevent us from our quiet celebration, rain especially, for then I cannot see her clearly across the courtyard. Too bright a sun is equally disruptive, because then the blind is drawn in her room. The best is a mellow sunlight, which lends itself to enhance her radiant beauty. *Pleni sunt coeli et terra gloria tua.* Her supply of flowery dresses seems simply inexhaustible, and with growing admiration and delight do I wait for every new revelation. Red blossoms, shining like so many setting suns, blue blossoms and yellow ones, fine lines of greenery spreading around the world. Red, blue, green; blueredredgreeeen. Redeeming bluety. Thou art bluetiful, o my love, out of thy perfection of bluety it shines.

Halleluja.

*

Palimpsests are an inheritance into which we are born like innocent babes unto an imperial throne. Their implications and responsibilities, impossibilities and ambiguities are with us from early childhood. Every pen-stroke has been made before, and every word on paper is barely legible among the innumerable former inscriptions and erasions. Even a newly invented word evokes in its similarities or through its contrast a multitude of unwanted relatives. To find the true sense of any word among the little black legs of the written centipedes which have grown through the centuries is a task so complex that the Communications, and the methods they extract from MS 62.7 Sem 3 are sorely needed if anything is to be accomplished. For this one needs the intuition of a poet. It is the terrible privilege of a poet not really to be part of human life, not to obey the ordinary rules of existence and its certainties. The word 'poeta' has always in this context fascinated and baffled me because it is so uncertain of its very gender, of its primary human condition (against this intuitionist theory it has been remarked that the same problem applies to *agricola*. This is true, but I ask leave to disregard this altogether; sometimes contradictions are all too ready at hand).

*

Priests bearing the ark of the covenant. This is how the editors have once been described by a colleague who is especially poetically minded, though he did not explain whether he said this in a spirit of flippancy or in all serious-ness. I somewhat doubt that it can be serious.

The terrible difficulty of the task of an editor is that he has not only to work on individual works, but also to distil the

rules for his work and its method out of the Communications of the Great Academy, which reach me continually
in the form of additions and sub-commentaries. Keeping up
with the reading is at times a challenging task in itself.
Malakh's repeated visits, always yielding yet another supplement, are received with different emotions ranging from
keenness to dismay, and indeed, when I look at the shelves
to my left – metres of volumes of the Communications,
their commentaries, auxiliary dictionaries, concordances – I
sometimes almost lose faith as to whether I can ever
manage the huge amount of literature which I am required
to know. Yet, at the bottom of the arguments of the Communications, there is the central idea, the method according
to which I must carry out the orders of Dr Javis, my
employer. The members of the Great Academy themselves
are most probably not aware of the central argument, so
much are they immersed in their discussions and dissent.
The argument has taken on a force which has long since
overtaken the importance of the simple questions or the
authority of Javis, who is formally the chairman of the
Academy. The Communications relate an amusing incident
which illustrates this point: in the Academy there was a
division over a relatively minor argument which split the
professors who were present into two opposed camps.
Javis, whose learning is immense, and who knows the
method, aligned himself with one of the parties and sup-
ported their line of thought. The Academy, however, would
not have it, and told him that, once he had given MS 62.7

Sem 3 into their hands and trusted their scholarship, it was entirely up to them to make all the decisions. He protested, and proved his point, but they would not hear him, and finally he gave up trying to press his argument. The academy is indeed so loyal that they do not surrender their responsibility to anyone, even to their founder. In the flurry and excitement of discussion, scholarly opinion and debate, the clear line of the argument seems often blurred, and exegetes, like my humble self, are dependent on commentaries and explanations in order to appreciate the fineries of the technical questions. Even if the process of establishing some points is often extremely trying, the joy I get from the study itself makes up for everything. Most edifying observations on history and ethics lie scattered among legal points like gems in a toolbox, and the sheer challenge of finding historical references and parallels of one case to another is a reward in itself. I do not hesitate to admit that the actual Dictionary, the individual files as such, have not yet received the attention they may deserve, nor in fact any attention for that matter. Cataloguing words, which superficially may seem the most important task, has admittedly not yet been undertaken by me to any extent which could be called systematic or comprehensive. Still, the preliminary work in which I am now engaged is much more important than mere mechanical classification. First the ideal method must be found, and only then can detail and procedures be dealt with.

Priest – or prisoner?

Chained to my task by regulations, I work away my time day after day. Barred from out there by walls of files and shelves of books, by barbed-letter-wire all around me, like Gulliver in Lilliput I live in this world of the second order, one step removed, always one step behind. Never-ending lines of small black words trail around me and keep me in my place. Beyond this nothing exists and so I try to make sense of the figures of the barbs in the long, long fences of my captivity, which are my guard and my sentence all at once. Thus I make new inches of wire, write myself deeper into my prison.

I do have little liberties, almost amounting to a little freedom. Like a prisoner who paces his cell on an imaginary journey around the world, I relish the subversion which the comedy staged on my picture in the dusk perpetuates on the alphabet, and every day I make an effort of self-determination, a conscious decision as to whether, how, and when I shall have my tea: Earl Grey or Darjeeling? Milk? Sugar?

My supreme and true freedom, however, is she, fairest among women.

Looking over at her is not a pursuit of superficial meaning in a world of little black-and-white devils. The free range of flowers on her dress defies every method and system, her beauty has no name. Were she to have one, she would become merely another file, another entry in the host of malignant and self-contradicting little words. Like this, it is a revelation proper, an unknown flowery dress in a mysterious room, an apparition of beauty, the name of which I am blissfully ignorant. Maybe it is only a piece of drapery which I see there, nothing more; then my Lady has indeed no name, is forever alive in my imagination only, safe from the tyranny of names and designations. Unattainable and radiant, she will be there, and I will raise my cup to her in a daily ritual of thanksgiving.

To her very good health.

*

Post-scriptum.

I have just received an editorial note from Malakh, summoning me finally to go and see Javis in his high office. I will go, despite the fact that I have the terrible idea that there may be nothing outside this room but empty illness and nagging grey normality. I will go and look for him, even if I discover that he is not there.

Farewell my Lady, beautiful apparition of glory!

*